THE ILLITERATE

A Novel

JIM FREED

Thought Catalog Books
Brooklyn, NY

THOUGHT CATALOG BOOKS

First edition, 2015
ISBN 978-0692554777
10 9 8 7 6 5 4 3 2 1

Founded in 2010, Thought Catalog is a website and imprint dedicated to your ideas and stories. We publish fiction and non-fiction from emerging and established writers across all genres.

Grateful acknowledgement is made to Special Rider Music for permission to reprint a lyric excerpt from "Ballad of a Thin Man," by Bob Dylan, copyright © 1965 by Warner Bros. Inc.; renewed 1993 by Special Rider Music. All rights reserved. International copyright secured. Reprinted by permission.

Cover art by © Mark Kupasrimonkol

For SWF and JFF

Well, you walk into the room
Like a camel and then you frown
You put your eyes in your pocket
And your nose on the ground
There ought to be a law
Against you comin' around
You should be made
To wear earphones

Because something is happening here
But you don't know what it is
Do you, Mister Jones?

    —Bob Dylan, "Ballad of a Thin Man"

CONTENTS

Chapter 1: Becoming the Illiterate   9

Chapter 2: At Work   14

Chapter 3: The Ophthalmologist   20

Chapter 4: The Girlfriend   36

Chapter 5: The Neurologist   55

Chapter 6: At Home   71

Chapter 7: The Psychiatrist   83

Chapter 8: Killing Time   99

Chapter 9: The Painter and The   116
Capitalist

Chapter 10: The Phone Calls   136

Chapter 11: At the Bar   153

Chapter 12: An Encounter with the   161
Conspirators

Chapter 13: At the Beach   173

Chapter 14: The Psychic   185

Chapter 15: The Ex-Detective   195

Chapter 16: Running the Gauntlet   214

Chapter 17: Escape from New York   220

Acknowledgements   225
About the Author   227

CHAPTER 1: BECOMING THE ILLITERATE

A little after 7 a.m. Jones heard his alarm go off. He hit the snooze button half a dozen times before opening his eyes. It was early March, but the weather was starting to turn for the better. The appeal of a spring day pulled Jones out of bed and into the shower. He listened to the news on the radio as he dressed and ate a quick breakfast of toast and coffee. Out on the street the wind was crisp, but the sun felt warm, and Jones walked happily to the train. He stopped at a bodega for a paper on the way.

On the subway platform, Jones unfolded his paper. But something was wrong with it. He could make out the photographs, but none of the words on the front page made sense: Instead of letters, he found strange marks on the newsprint that didn't resemble anything he'd ever seen. He leafed through it and found a similar collection of ink blobs and broken lines on each page. *Is this a joke?* Jones thought. *Or maybe a fluke at the printing press?* These possibilities struck him as funny and even absurd, but now he had a 45-minute commute with nothing to read! Jones was annoyed that he hadn't noticed the paper's defect in the store. He'd have to hold on to it and stop by the bodega on his way home from work for a refund.

When the train arrived it was already crowded. Jones pushed his way onto it. He tried to forget about the paper; a serious man like him didn't have time for things like a paper with only pictures. That's what he told himself. Once the train was in motion, Jones tried to concentrate on the day before him. Emerging from the tunnel onto the Manhattan Bridge, it hit him that he was not only a serious man, but a successful one too. Just seven years earlier he'd moved to New York to be a writer, and this is what he had become. He'd recently finished his first novel, and he held an editorial position at a reputable culturally centered newsmagazine that inspired envy in his artistic-minded peers. Jones was proud of what he had achieved, and on this fine morning he felt his pride swell.

Then the train slammed on its brakes. It was just a few feet away from the entrance to the tunnel into Manhattan. *What now?* Jones thought.

According to the announcement that followed, due to a situation with a sick passenger at the station ahead, the train would bypass it and make local stops. Jones looked up to the subway map to calculate the number of additional stops, but something was wrong. He could see a bunch of small lights indicating the stops, but he couldn't read the names of the stations. Instead Jones saw a strange series of shapes and broken lines similar to what he'd seen in his paper. *Vandalism?* he thought. Jones pushed his way through the crowded train car to check another map. He recognized the lines and the colors on the map but still couldn't read the words. He rubbed his eyes and thought maybe he'd put in a defective pair of contact lenses. He leaned closer to the map to get a better look, but then a hand pushed against his chest. He looked down and saw an old man wearing thick glasses staring at him.

Excuse me, son, said the old man. You mind giving me some room? I'm sorry, said Jones. I'm just trying to figure out where to get off. Where are you going? asked the old man. Times Square, said Jones. The old man pivoted toward the map and pointed to it. Well, right now we're here and you're going there, said the old man, pointing at a location on the map where all the colored lines intersected. Jones recognized this as his destination, but he still couldn't decipher the station name or any of the words on the map. But how do you know that? asked Jones. Because it says so right here, said the old man. But it doesn't say a goddamn thing, said Jones. Excuse me? said the old man. The words on the map, said Jones. Son, I think you'd better take a step back, said the old man. I can't read any of the words, said Jones. What's the matter with you? asked the old man. I just told you, said Jones. For some reason I can't read the words. Are you on the drugs, son? asked the old man. Jones looked down at the old man and noticed how thick his glasses were. You wouldn't mind if I borrow those for a second? asked Jones. He reached for the man's glasses without waiting for his answer. He put them on and looked at the map but still couldn't make out a single letter. Jones would have liked to have examined it more closely, but before he had a chance he felt a blow to the right side of his face that sent his head into a pole. The old man took back his glasses and pushed Jones into the other passengers. What the hell's wrong with you? he yelled. Someone grab him! Call the police!

Jones spun away from the man. The crowd looked at him with disgust. Jones didn't know what to do. The train was pulling into a station. Across the platform Jones spotted another train, so he decided to make a break for it. Once the train stopped, he pushed his way through the other passengers and sprinted across the platform onto the train. *Just my lucky day,* Jones thought. The doors closed behind him.

The train was nearly empty. Jones slumped down into a seat and tried to pull himself together. He couldn't believe he had almost assaulted an old man. The conductor announced the next stop, and Jones realized he only had two more to go. He looked up at the map, but once again he saw only lights and lines and couldn't decipher the words. Jones felt his heart beat faster and he slammed his fist into the bench. He needed to remain calm. He tried to breathe slower and more deeply. He would get to his stop soon. He would go into work and figure something out.

At the next stop a few people entered his car. At first Jones didn't notice them, but then he heard a voice. Someone was reading. He looked up and saw a young woman sitting across from him with her toddler, who was in a stroller. She was reading from a book, maybe Dr. Seuss. The child enjoyed this immensely and Jones enjoyed it as well. She assumed a different voice for each character and as she read Jones couldn't help watching them. He hoped he wasn't staring. Jones especially couldn't resist stealing glances at the kid. She was a little girl no older than two or three, with curly blonde hair. Jones found peace sitting there watching the toddler enjoy the book. But then the woman stopped reading.

Jones looked up at her. Can I help you with something? she asked. I don't think so, said Jones. Sir, I'm sorry if my reading to my daughter disturbed you, she continued. I actually enjoyed it, said Jones. Excuse me? said the woman. Then Jones looked into the woman's eyes and saw that she was afraid. Seeing her like this made him nervous. I'm sorry, said Jones. I guess I recognized what you read. Perhaps from my own childhood? What's the title? She held the book up to him, but he couldn't make out any of the words. Maybe you could just tell me what it is? said Jones. He looked back at the little girl. She was starting to fuss. What's wrong with you? said the woman. Can't you read?

The woman comforted her child. Jones looked down at the floor in shame. He anxiously waited for the subway doors to open as the train pulled into the next station.

CHAPTER 2: AT WORK

Once Jones reached his office he found the spare pair of contact lenses he kept in his desk and headed to the bathroom. Replacing the lenses seemed to make no difference, so he took out the new pair and looked at the newspaper with his naked eyes. It was still blurry, so he held it up close. The shapes came into focus, but still no words. Jones stuck his head into the sink and flushed his eyes with water. He'd been nearsighted his entire life and often took out his contacts when he read. The sharpening of the text confirmed his disability but said nothing of this new inability. *How strange,* Jones thought. He held his eyelids open under the running water. After about a minute of this, Jones put his contact lenses back in and looked at the newspaper. Nothing had changed. He was still illiterate.

Jones went back to his office and sat at his desk. He pulled out a pad of paper and wrote "I have become an illiterate" across the top of it and watched his hand make a series of disjointed lines and strange circles that his eyes didn't recognize. Then he wrote "I have become an illiterate" again, and he saw the exact same shapes. *Well, well,* Jones thought, *at least there seems to be a semblance of order to all this madness.* Then just to be certain he wasn't mistaken Jones wrote "I have become an illiterate" one last time and saw a series of shapes identical to the first two lines.

He needed to see a doctor at once.

This seemed like something an ophthalmologist would handle so Jones turned on his computer to look for one. Google was his homepage, so he relied on his memory to type "ophthalmologist" and "10018" into the search engine. Seconds later the results came up, but Jones should have known better: He couldn't make out a single word. He tried clicking on a few links, hoping he would automatically send an email, but nothing took him where he wanted to go. He grew frustrated and figured he'd be better off asking his assistant for help. He picked up the phone and asked her to come to his office.

Jones hung up and looked at the keypad. He remembered the position of the numbers on the phone, but he couldn't make out any of the digits. They looked the same to him as letters; where each number should have been he saw only broken lines and mismatched shapes. Jones glanced at his cell phone and found it was the same.

Good morning, sir, said the assistant, as she approached his desk. Good morning, said Jones. Why don't you pull up a chair?

The assistant wheeled over a chair from the meeting table by the window in the corner of Jones's office. As she walked toward him with the chair, Jones noticed she was wearing a tight leather skirt and suddenly felt incredibly turned on. For a few seconds, Jones fantasized about taking her right there on his desk. *No, no, that'll have to happen another time,* Jones thought as she sat down next to him. And then: *What the hell is wrong with me? To even think about such a thing at a time like this?* Listen, said Jones, this morning has been one of the strangest I've ever had. I'm going to need your help with something. OK, said the assistant. More or less it's just a small project, said Jones. And the thing is, I want to apologize for asking you what I'm about to ask you in advance, because I'm sure this is going to sound ridiculous. You see, it's just that…, Jones started to say. Yes? said the assistant. Well, I'm afraid I can't read anymore, said Jones. What? said the assistant. It's true, said Jones. Somehow it seems I've become illiterate. I'm not sure I understand what you mean, said the assistant. Words don't mean anything to me anymore, said Jones. For instance, take this newspaper. Jones picked up his paper and showed it to her. All I see are pictures and blobs of ink, said Jones. Well, I have to agree with you there, said the assistant, smiling. You agree? said Jones. Today's papers really are in a sordid state of affairs, she said. That's why I work for you and this wonderful magazine! But that's not what I mean at all, said Jones. Frustrated, he picked up the piece of paper he had been writing on before the assistant came to his desk and passed it over to her. What does this paper say? asked Jones. The assistant looked down at the paper and then back at him and then back down at the paper. She seemed confused. Well, it says "I have become an illiterate." It says "I have become an illiterate" three times. Yes, said Jones, grinning. But you see, when I look at it, I don't see anything but broken links and blobs of ink. How can that be? said the assistant. Clearly it's your handwriting. It certainly is, said Jones. I just wrote it a few minutes ago. But something strange has happened. At first I thought there was something wrong with my contacts, so I took them out and cleaned them. As far as

I can tell, they seem to be functioning fine, so now I'm thinking it might be my optic nerve or maybe my brain? Like maybe I had a stroke or something? How did you write this, then? asked the assistant. How is that possible, if it's true you've become an illiterate? I remember how to write, said Jones. I guess I've been writing so long that even if I can't see the words I'm writing, I still remember how to move my hand. After I got in today the first thing I did was search for a nearby ophthalmologist on the Internet, but I can't make out any of the results on the screen. Really? said the assistant. I need you to find me a good doctor, said Jones, and make me an appointment for as soon as possible. Right away, said the assistant. If anyone comes around looking for me tell them I'm out sick, said Jones. Of course, said the assistant. But what should I tell the editor? He's already been by asking about that feature you owe him today.

At the mention of his boss, Jones sank deeper in his chair. The night before, he'd been up late working on a review of a recently released novel by one of the country's most respected writers. It was his aim to write it in an extremely idiosyncratic style that would distinguish his piece from the other reviews and possibly even signal to the writer in question that he was the sort of up-and-coming writer the renowned author should keep his eye on. He'd tried a number of different approaches, but nothing read as he wanted it to, so he saved each version on his flash drive and planned to review them in the morning and write a new version for his editor first thing.

If you haven't written it yet, you could dictate it to me, said the assistant. Jones considered the idea for a moment, but decided against it because he wasn't sure he could trust her to type what he told her and his new condition prevented him from reviewing her work. He thanked her for the offer, and told her to just start calling doctors. As for his review, he would figure something out.

*

What a strange joke life seems to be playing on me, Jones thought. He didn't understand why this illiteracy had happened on that particular day. A week before, he'd been given the chance to write something that could potentially distinguish him and advance his career. Now his copy was due and he had nothing. *But what do I still have?* Jones thought about the dozens of approaches he'd tried the night before. Maybe it was just a matter of recalling these ideas and pasting them together as best he could? And then, before he really knew what he wanted to write, Jones placed his fingers on his keyboard, closed his eyes, and started working. He tried to keep journalistic structure in mind, but there was no turning back. At times he was positive his prose was just a series of disjointed digressions. But he didn't let himself get hung up on these thoughts; Jones kept typing because that was the only thing he *could* do. After an hour or two, he felt certain he had exhausted everything he had to say, so he saved his work and printed it. He tried to email a copy to his editor, but he wasn't sure if it went through and he didn't care.

Jones stood up and collected his things. He grabbed the printout and took it to the assistant's desk. He asked her to give the review to his editor, and she told him the address of an ophthalmologist with whom she'd arranged his appointment, set to start in half an hour. Is there anything else I can do for you? asked the assistant. No, said Jones. Well, good luck, said the assistant. Thanks, said Jones. Then he turned away from her and headed out of the office.

CHAPTER 3: THE OPHTHALMOLOGIST

The ophthalmologist's office was much farther away than Jones expected it to be. Each time he asked a passerby for directions, he was assured he was close, but needed to head a bit farther west. Jones tried his best to remain optimistic. He was frustrated, but it was a pleasant day and he enjoyed watching the streetscape change from the office towers of midtown into the blue-collar bars and crumbling brownstones of Hell's Kitchen. At some corners Jones was tempted to ditch his appointment and stop by one of the watering holes for a drink instead. *But there is important business to attend to,* he thought, *the very important business of finding out why I woke up unable to read.*

Eventually Jones hit the West Side Highway. *Could I have missed it?* he thought. Something wasn't right. He took out his cell phone and called his assistant. He asked her to call the doctor's office and verify the address. She put him on hold. While he was waiting he noticed two kids about half a block away fighting. They were probably 12 or 13 years old. One kid looked sort of big and the other one seemed a little small. Jones wasn't sure what to do. He didn't know if it was his responsibility as an adult to intervene. He certainly didn't want to. It was a stupid kid fight. They were just pushing each other. The little guy was quicker, but the bigger kid was almost twice his size. Suddenly the little one lunged into the bigger kid and sent him flying into a pile of trash. *What a feisty little fucker,* Jones thought. The smaller kid took off and the bigger kid was after him a second later. Jones lost track of them after a block or two.

The assistant came back on the line and told Jones that he was headed to the office of Dr. Floyd, on the ground floor of a brownstone between 11th Avenue and the highway. The building's exterior was fire engine red and on the stoop were two pots of fake geraniums colored red, white, and blue. Jones thanked his assistant and headed back toward 11th Avenue. He found the red brownstone with the fake geraniums half a block away. A few of the pots had little windmills stuck in with the plants.

*

The reception area of Dr. Floyd's office was cramped and smelled of mildew. The carpet was ragged, as if it hadn't been changed in decades, and the tiny room was filled with mismatched furniture that looked like it had been salvaged from the street. An elderly couple wearing heavy overcoats sat just inside the door. The old man wore thick glasses and Jones thought he noticed a teardrop rolling down his face. The woman, his wife Jones presumed, sat next to him stroking his hand. Jones nodded to them as he entered the room, but neither responded. Both were watching a small television on the other side of the room. Jones took a glance at it as he approached the reception window. It was tuned to a soap opera.

Jones saw the receptionist seated near the back of a small office on the other side of the window. Excuse me, he said. But she didn't respond. Miss? Jones said. Still, she remained silent. Jones wasn't sure what to do. He stared at her. She appeared to be filing her nails. Jones tried to get her attention again. He cleared his throat as abrasively as he could. The elderly couple turned away from the television and glared at him. But the receptionist continued to ignore him. He started tapping his fingers on the wooden frame of the window. Then he noticed a bell hidden under some medical forms to his left and rang it. The receptionist wheeled her chair over to the window at once. *What a ridiculous old bitch,* Jones thought. For a second he considered letting her have it, but decided it would be more tactful to keep his mouth shut until after he had seen the doctor.

Can I help you? said the receptionist. Yes, said Jones. I have an appointment with the ophthalmologist. You have an appointment? said the receptionist. Yes, said Jones. Well let's see, she said, looking into what he imagined was an appointment book, though after a minute went by and she didn't look back up at him he reasoned that it was just as possible she was reading a magazine. Listen, said Jones. Is this Dr. Floyd's office? It is, said the receptionist. Dr. Floyd the ophthalmologist? asked Jones. Yes, of course, said the receptionist. Well that's who I've come to see, said Jones. My assistant called an hour ago and made me an appointment. In fact she just called a few minutes ago to ask for directions. Of course, said the receptionist, what a nice young lady. Yes, said Jones, she's invaluable to me. She had such a nice voice, said the receptionist. There's something so confident, yet seductive about it. I suppose you're right, said Jones. But look, is the doctor in? Yes, of course, said the receptionist. I'll just need you to fill out some forms. She placed a clipboard on the counter. Jones looked back at her and frowned. Is there a problem, sir? said the receptionist. Yes, said Jones. I know this will sound ridiculous, but right now I can't fill out these forms. And why is that? said the receptionist. Well, you see, said Jones, the reason I've come to see the doctor today is because this morning I woke up unable to read. Sir, said the receptionist, I'm afraid you'll have to take up all medical questions with the doctor. But how am I supposed to fill out medical forms if I can't read what they say? said Jones. Sir, said the receptionist, I'm not sure how to answer that. Well I guess I'll just try to complete them the best I can, said Jones. He took the clipboard from the receptionist and sat down.

Jones looked at the forms. Beyond a few images that seemed to be official medical seals, all he could make out were blurred ink and broken lines. *Why don't people listen to me?* he wondered. *Is it entirely impossible for people to believe what I say?* He felt enraged. He flipped over the forms and wrote:

> I woke up this morning unable to read letters or numbers, but otherwise my vision seems unharmed. For example I can still see pictures clearly. I am still able to write because I am a professional writer so it's my assumption that out of habit my hands still remember how to form letters. My current disability makes it impossible for me to fill out these medical forms. I would be happy to answer any questions you might have orally.

Jones stood up and passed the clipboard back to the receptionist. She read what he wrote and rolled her eyes. Please be seated, she said. I'll let the doctor know you're here. Then she stood up with the clipboard and walked through a small door in the back of the reception booth.

Jones sat back down and started paging through one of the magazines he spotted on the table in front of him, but he was done in a matter of minutes. *If only they had National Geographic,* he thought. He looked through the stack of magazines for something with more pictures, but he didn't find anything. Eventually Jones started watching the soap opera with the elderly couple. The story line seemed to be about a love triangle gone wrong that leads to murder, but it might have been about a lost child or a squandered inheritance as well. He wasn't certain, but it didn't really matter. The actresses were gorgeous in a sort of hot and trashy way, and all it took was a minute or two before Jones felt a slight erection coming on. *Nice nicety nice,* he thought. *Maybe waiting here won't be so bad after all.*

A door suddenly opened. On impulse Jones stood up. He assumed the doctor had come for him, but it was actually just the door to the street, so Jones sat back down. A boy walked into the room. At first Jones just nodded to him and turned back to the soap opera, but then he realized it was the bigger kid from the fight on the street. Now the boy was wearing a ridiculously large pair of dark glasses. He walked past Jones and the elderly couple to the reception window. He reached up and rang the bell. Then he rang it again, and again, and again. The elderly couple hissed at him to be quiet, but the boy ignored them and continued ringing the bell. He went on like that for nearly a minute. Then he picked up a magazine and took a seat across from Jones. Sorry if I disturbed you, said the boy, but the bitch always takes forever. Don't worry about it, said Jones. I'm not really watching, but you may have bothered these folks. Well I don't give a flying fuck about them, said the boy. Then he stood back up and hit the bell a dozen more times before sitting down again. I bet the bitch is back there banging out the doc. Every time I come here they're going at it. Dr. Floyd? said Jones. He's one creepy old fuck, said the boy. So you're a regular patient then? said Jones. You bet, said the boy. I come here once a week. This place is the worst, but it beats going to school. I guess you must have something seriously wrong with your eyes? said Jones. Take a look for yourself, he said. The little boy raised his dark glasses. His eyes were glassy and pale. Then he pulled his glasses back down. What happened to you? said Jones. I burnt my eyes out looking into the sun, said the boy. Jesus! said Jones. Was it that little twerp who held you down? Huh? said the boy. When I was walking over here I think I may have seen you being bullied by a smaller boy, said Jones. Oh, little Ralphie? said the boy. Fuck no. What you saw on your way over here was a function of what some call karma. Karma? said Jones. In what way? You see, I used to be the bully in this here neighborhood. I used to terrorize all the kids from around here for years. And now everyone terrorizes you? said Jones. Well I certainly had it coming, but there's a little more to it than that. You see once I started getting older I realized I'd never be good at school. I also realized that most of the people I'd picked on were smarter than me and I figured it was only a matter of time before they'd try to get back at me by calling me stupid, which would make me get back at them by messing with them even more. OK? said Jones. But through the example of my old man, I learned that this sort of bullying inevitably leads to physical violence, which in my case leads to jail. You see my dad's been in and out of the joint his entire life, and personally it doesn't sound too appealing. He was your typical repeat offender destined to die in a cage. But then something happened that changed his life. Really? said Jones. Yeah, said the boy. One day he got injured on a construction job he had when he was out on parole. Now he collects disability and lives like a king. No kidding, said Jones. And the way I saw things, if I was going to follow in my old man's footsteps that would entail decades of physical violence, psychological torment, and recurring incarceration. You really are quite an insightful young man, said Jones. So I figured why not just cut to the chase and get myself my own disability while I'm young and still have a chance to enjoy my life. I'm sorry? said Jones. You see, the boy continued, burning my eyes out staring into the sun was relatively painless. My old man only got disability after a whole truck full of bricks fell on him and now the fucker can hardly walk. And even though it was an accident, the fuckers at the disability bureau had the nerve to suggest that his injury may have been deliberate because he didn't want to work. But with me, I'm just a stupid little kid and stupid little kids do stupid shit all the time so no one's going to question me. But how badly is your eyesight damaged? asked Jones. It's fucked up, but not entirely, said the boy. I can't really read anymore but I never liked reading all that much. I've always been more of a movies/television kind of guy. But that's insane, said Jones. Is it? said the boy. You said you blinded yourself to get out of having to endure a painful life, said Jones, but just today I saw you getting your ass kicked by a little twerp. So what? said the boy. Well, that must have been painful, said Jones. It's got to be difficult for you to let yourself get pushed around like that? Man, I know this will sound sort of ridiculous, said the boy, but it's calculated karma. Calculated karma? said Jones. Listen,

I'm 13 years old right now. I could potentially get hassled by the kids I fucked with for the next five years. That sounds shitty, but it's not that bad when you consider that I've been fucking with them for the past eight years. And it seems even less shitty when you figure that a lot of kids lose interest in vengeance and all that crap as they grow up, and less shittier still when you consider that once I turn 18 the state hooks my motherfucking ass up. Well I guess I didn't think of it like that, said Jones. Well glad to have broadened your horizons, brother, said the boy. And besides what you saw today with Ralphie, man that's all show. Sometimes I even let him think he's hurting me. Really? said Jones. Yeah, said the boy, because I mean it's all nothing to me. Fuck the present and the past. The way I see things, it's all about the future. Good point, said Jones. Unless you don't have one, like these fucks, the boy continued, pointing to the elderly couple. Look, I think she's trying to give him a hand job. He nodded toward the old man's pants. Jones looked over to the couple. The old woman had her hand inside the man's pocket. The man's eyes were shut tightly as if he were trying to concentrate on something far, far away. Dare me to fish it out? said the boy. Before Jones had a chance to answer him, the boy stood up and started tiptoeing toward the man.

Jones figured that he should probably stop him, but at the same time he was sort of curious if the boy would actually go through with it. *This kid sure has some balls,* Jones thought. A door opened and the receptionist stepped into the room. The kid froze. Martin, said the receptionist, you behave yourself and leave Mr. and Mrs. Callahan alone. He backed away from the old man and sat down. The receptionist turned to Jones. Sir, the doctor will see you now.

*

The corridor leading to the doctor's office was nearly pitch black. With each step the smell of mildew grew stronger and it became harder for Jones to breathe. He couldn't help thinking that perhaps he had offended his assistant in the office that morning. *Out of all the ophthalmologists in the city, to end up in a place like this,* Jones thought.

Finally Jones spotted a dim light ahead. It was coming from behind a door that was cracked open. He knocked, but no one answered, so he knocked again, harder this time, and accidentally caused the door to swing open. Inside, Jones found a cramped examination room. There was a large chair in the center with an examination instrument suspended above it. Hello? said Jones. Is anyone here? He stepped into the room. He noticed a little old man sitting at a small desk in the corner. Large tufts of white hair protruded from both of his ears. He was writing frantically on a yellow legal pad. As if on cue the man spun around on the stool he was sitting on and faced Jones. Ah, hello sir, said the man. Please come in and have a seat. Dr. Floyd? said Jones. He sat down in the examining chair. At your service, said the ophthalmologist. I apologize for the delay, but we had to squeeze you in last minute. Sorry for not scheduling this more in advance, said Jones. I didn't realize anything was wrong until this morning. I had my assistant make me this appointment as soon as I got to work. And what work do you do? asked the ophthalmologist. I'm a writer, said Jones. A writer? said the ophthalmologist. Yes, said Jones.

What kind do you do? asked the ophthalmologist. Well, I just finished a novel and am in the process of trying to sell it, said Jones. Congratulations, said the ophthalmologist. Thanks, said Jones. But I support myself by writing journalism. Ah, said the ophthalmologist, the artist and the practical man in one. I suppose you could say that, said Jones. In my youth I wanted to be a writer, said the ophthalmologist. Really? said Jones. Yes, said the ophthalmologist, but after my efforts met only failure, I decided to go to med school instead. Well the writer's life can be a difficult one, said Jones. Of course, said the ophthalmologist. But take it from me, med school wasn't a field day. Of course not, said Jones. I think it's fair to say that each man's life is tough in its own way, said the ophthalmologist. That's true, said Jones. But often I wonder what would have happened if I had tried to be a writer just a little longer, said the ophthalmologist. Do you still write today? asked Jones. I do, actually, said the ophthalmologist. I've never been able to shake the writer bug. That's great, said Jones. In fact, just as you came in now I was working on my novel. The ophthalmologist picked up the yellow legal pad from his desk and held it up for Jones to see. What's it about? said Jones. You know how it is, said the ophthalmologist, it's hard to say. I understand completely, said Jones. But basically it's about an arsonist who takes on the world, said the ophthalmologist. That's interesting, said Jones. Yes, said the ophthalmologist. It's an idea that interests me greatly. Well best of luck completing it, said Jones. Thank you, said the ophthalmologist. You know, I'm sure you're a busy man and you get this all the time, but would you mind taking a look at what I've written? Well, doctor, Jones started to say. You wouldn't even need to look at the entire thing, said the ophthalmologist. It's just I've been out of the game for quite some time so having a real writer's opinion of my work would be invaluable. Of course, said Jones. Perhaps you wouldn't mind taking a quick glance at what I was working on just now? I wouldn't mind at all, said Jones, but right now I'm afraid I can't. You can't? said the ophthalmologist. Under normal circumstances I would gladly look at your work and give you my opinion. But I can't read your prose or anything else today. That's precisely why I came to see you! Is that supposed to be your way of telling me you don't think I have what it takes to be a writer? said the ophthalmologist. Of course not, said Jones. If you really don't want to read it, you could have just said no, said the ophthalmologist. But I'd love to read it, said Jones. You know, it's not polite to be indirect with strangers, said the ophthalmologist. I realize this, said Jones, but I'm not trying to be rude. I woke up this morning unable to read letters or numbers! So you say here in this note, said the ophthalmologist. He was reading Jones's file. But you still possess the ability to write? Well writing is more of a habit, said Jones. It's something I do without thinking about it. I bet it is, said the ophthalmologist. Excuse me? said Jones. Do you really expect me to believe all this? asked the ophthalmologist. Do you think I would have come to see you if I wasn't serious? said Jones. How should I know that? said the ophthalmologist. Excuse me? asked Jones. I don't know you, said the ophthalmologist. How should I know what your agenda is? But you're a doctor, said Jones. As far as I know you could be some sneaky journalist looking for a scandal to break, said the ophthalmologist. That's absurd, said Jones. Or maybe one of my enemies has paid you to try to tarnish my reputation, said the ophthalmologist. Why would one of your associates wish to do such a thing? asked Jones. Well I am known for being somewhat of an eccentric, said the ophthalmologist. I assure you, the only reason I came to see you today is because I seem to have lost my ability to read and am extremely concerned about my condition, said Jones. Well I'd hope you'd be, said the ophthalmologist. Some romanticize illiteracy, you know? Some see it as the end-all cure. Who would think a thing like that? asked Jones. Perhaps you happened to meet young Martin in the waiting room? Who? asked Jones. The boy sitting out there now wearing the large sunglasses? The stupid little shit who burned out his retinas staring into the sun? Yes, said Jones, I did speak with him. A strange boy, but he did make some interesting points. Interesting indeed! said the ophthalmologist. The boy is so proud of his little accident. He didn't like school or reading so the idiot stared into the sun because he thought that would make his life easier. But what the little shit doesn't realize is that when he begins to receive his treasured disability payments he will have most likely gone completely blind. Have you told him this? asked Jones. Of course not, said the ophthalmologist. But you're his doctor, said Jones. Yes, said the ophthalmologist. It will be a wonderful day when he finally understands what he's done. But my god, that's sadistic, said Jones. I only bring up the boy because I can't think of a better cautionary tale, said the ophthalmologist. Learn from his stupidity and stop doing what ever you've begun to do to yourself before it's too late. But I haven't done anything, said Jones. Well what happened then? asked the ophthalmologist. I already told you, said Jones. I woke up this morning unable to read. Do you have any medical conditions? asked the ophthalmologist. No, said Jones. Have you had any serious diseases? No, said Jones. Any recent injuries or head trauma? No, said Jones. Ever experience double vision? Never, said Jones. Ever have any other major vision problems? I've worn glasses and contacts nearly my entire life, said Jones. Is there anything I should know before I examine you? the ophthalmologist continued. I don't think so, said Jones. Before today I've never had any health problems. In fact right now I feel like I'm in the best shape of my entire life. Do you drink? asked the ophthalmologist? Just socially, said Jones. Do you take any prescription drugs? said the ophthalmologist. No, said Jones. What about recreational ones? said the ophthalmologist. Well, said Jones, every now and then I smoke a little pot. So you're a habitual smoker of marijuana? said the ophthalmologist. I suppose you could say that, said Jones. It relaxes me. What about hard drugs? said the ophthalmologist. Hard drugs? said Jones. Don't tell me you haven't heard of them, said the ophthalmologist with a chuckle. Have you ever taken heroin, methamphetamines, PCP, or cocaine? I only ask because anything you have voluntarily ingested could be a potential cause of your current condition. I see, said Jones. Well occasionally, like very occasionally, I do a little coke. So you infrequently snort cocaine? said the ophthalmologist. He made a note in Jones's file. I do, said Jones, but only on rare occasions. Like on New Year's Eve. Well that's a dirty little habit, said the ophthalmologist. I don't do drugs regularly, said Jones. I don't do any more than anyone else I know. I can't say I haven't heard that one before, said the ophthalmologist. Excuse me? said Jones. People like you make me sick, said the ophthalmologist. What are you talking about? said Jones.

Here you are living the dream, said the ophthalmologist. You've got a finished novel and support yourself through writing professionally, but you still snort a little coke every now and then. And now here you are in my lousy little office telling me you woke up unable to read. But I'm telling the truth, said Jones. You have to believe me!

The ophthalmologist flipped off the lights and switched on a projector. Rows of what Jones assumed to be various sized letters appeared on the wall in front of him, though all he could make out were a series of differently sized broken lines and shapes. Please read the first line you can, said the ophthalmologist. But that's just the problem, said Jones. The lines I see are in focus but I can't read a thing. If you can't tell me which letters you can read, how do you expect me to gauge your ability to see? said the ophthalmologist. Dr. Floyd, I am being absolutely honest with you, said Jones. I cannot read a single letter. Surely you must have another way to test if my eyes have been damaged? There is the kiddie chart, said the ophthalmologist. Perfect, said Jones. The ophthalmologist switched out the transparency on the projector with another. It contained numerous lines of colored shapes varying in size. What is the smallest line you can read? asked the ophthalmologist. Jones read the smallest one he could make out. If you can see that, said the ophthalmologist, with your contacts in your vision is 20/15. But what about my vision up close? asked Jones. We'll test that now, said the ophthalmologist. The doctor asked Jones to take out his contacts and read another series of shapes up close, and once again Jones had no difficulty doing what the doctor asked. According to the tests you have perfect vision, said the ophthalmologist. But how can that be? asked Jones. Just to be certain, I'll examine your retinas too. The ophthalmologist gave Jones some drops to dilate his pupils. He told him he would be back in a few minutes once the drops had a chance to kick in.

Jones waited for his pupils to dilate. He thought about the day and how strange it had been. His life had changed so quickly. *Maybe it's fate?* he thought. *Maybe it's the universe's way of telling me I should give up writing all together? Because, as the doctor said, I have ruined myself.* He didn't know what to think. He just couldn't believe it.

A few minutes later the ophthalmologist returned to the room. He asked Jones to put his chin up onto an instrument. The ophthalmologist looked through it and examined each of Jones's eyes. Eventually he pushed away the machine and flipped on the light. Jones winced and squinted. Oh, sorry, said the ophthalmologist. You won't really be able to see anything until your pupils shrink back down to size. He handed Jones a small pair of disposable sunglasses. Jones put them on. Did you see anything out of the ordinary? said Jones. No, said the ophthalmologist. As far as I can tell you have nothing wrong with your eyes. But how can that be possible? said Jones. I really don't know what to say, said the ophthalmologist. Here are some drops. He handed Jones a small plastic bottle. If you have any sort of infection they should take care of it. If you don't, the drops won't harm you. But why can't I read? asked Jones. I don't know, said the ophthalmologist. For now I think you need to go home and get some rest. If you're still having trouble reading tomorrow you're welcome to give me a call. You also might want to consider seeing a neurologist. A neurologist? said Jones. Yes, said the ophthalmologist. You should consider having someone take a look at your optic nerve. That's located in your brain. There's a chance what has happened to you could be quite serious. What could it be? asked Jones. I'm not sure, said the ophthalmologist. I can refer you to a neurologist who specializes in optic issues if you'd like? I'd be grateful, said Jones. But I won't be able to read the name and number you write down for me. Very well, said the ophthalmologist. I'll ask my receptionist to schedule an appointment for you some time tomorrow. She'll tell you where you need to be. You can always call if you have any questions. OK, thanks, said Jones. You're welcome, said the ophthalmologist. Then he shook his head. Just do yourself a favor and stay away from the drugs. Of course, said Jones. You do realize that junk puts holes in your brain? said the ophthalmologist. I think I've heard something like that, said Jones. Just look at yourself, said the ophthalmologist. One day you're a promising young talent and the next you're a confused illiterate. You should be ashamed.

*

Jones walked back down the dark corridor. When he got to the waiting room the receptionist told him that she had made him an appointment with the neurologist for the following day at noon. She read him the address over and over again until he memorized it and then gave him a piece of paper where she had written it down just in case he forgot it and needed to ask for directions. Then Jones thanked her and walked out the door.

CHAPTER 4: THE GIRLFRIEND

As he walked out of the ophthalmologist's office Jones remembered he had plans to spend the evening with his girlfriend and decided to head over to her place right away. It was already 5 o'clock. After the day he'd had, he felt drained and he couldn't bear the thought of going back to his office or facing his assistant, so he called his girlfriend. She was delighted to see him earlier than they had originally planned and asked him to pick up two bottles of wine she'd been dying to try. *Ah,* Jones thought, *despite everything that has happened, some things remain the same. My dear little Caroline still has such particular and cultivated tastes.* Knowing that it was likely he would forget the names of the wines she wanted before he got to the store, Jones found a pen and a scrap of paper in his pocket and wrote them down.

Jones felt a renewed sense of confidence as he walked to the subway. He'd had a strange day. But he had done everything he could to address his odd condition. And now there he was on his way to spend the evening with the woman he loved. There he was walking away from the city that had given him everything. What did he care if on that particular day the city had decided to take something away? So what if it had taken away his ability to read?

Naturally Jones should regard this as nothing more than a test, one among the many tests that he had always excelled on in the past. That was that. Things were settled. That night he would rest and the next day he would figure out everything.

Jones found a certain peace in these thoughts. He began to feel like his old self for the first time all day. But these thoughts must have distracted him too. Just seconds later he had the lousy luck of walking straight into a pay phone. The impact knocked him down. *How could I have not seen that?* Jones wondered. He sat up on the sidewalk and rubbed his head. Are you OK, sir? he heard someone say above him. And then: Mister? Damn, you see that guy eat it? Sir, are you OK? Do you need me to call 911? No, I'm fine, said Jones. He looked up at the people gathered around him. Oddly, though, he seemed unable to make out any details on the faces before him and instead saw only black blotches. *Just perfect*, Jones thought. *Now have I become blind as well?* But then Jones remembered that the ophthalmologist dilated his pupils. That fucker! Jones yelled. The circle of people gathered around him backed away. Sir, said one man, do you require medical attention? No, said Jones. I just left the eye doctor. I had my pupils dilated. I can't see that well right now. Just give me a minute. Whatever you say, drunky, said another. Please just leave me alone and let me sit here for a moment, said Jones. Do you need anything? another man said. Maybe some water? said Jones. I'll get it, sir, said a boy standing close by. Jones fished a few dollars out of his pocket and gave the kid the money. Thanks, he said. Any time, said the boy. Then Jones watched the little bastard run away. The crowd standing around him didn't seem shocked at all. One person leaned in and told Jones that he should be more careful with his money.

Eventually someone helped him to his feet and Jones continued walking to the train. He went much slower now and tried to be more cautious. The effects of the drops the ophthalmologist had used were much stronger than he thought they'd be. The sun was just starting to set and the city was filled with millions of crisscrossing yellow lines. Jones walked directly into a sunray. He winced in pain. His eyes burned. *I guess they're just sensitive to the light?* he thought. The disposable sunglasses he wore didn't seem to be helping much, so he lowered them, but when he did the light stung his eyes again. The faces of the people passing by him on the street blurred when they got close and it all became too disorienting to bear. He put the glasses back on and did his best to not bump into anything else. Once he reached the subway entrance he eagerly descended into the darkness below.

*

The subway platform was packed with the rush hour crowd. At first Jones found it difficult to maneuver past all the people under the glare of the fluorescent lights overhead. But he took his time and before long found himself on a train speeding east toward the remote part of Brooklyn where his girlfriend lived. The trip would take him nearly an hour. One man noticed Jones's disposable sunglasses and offered him his seat. I hate going to the eye doctor, he said. Tell me about it, said Jones, I can hardly see a thing. Then with a nod their conversation ended and once again Jones was left alone with his thoughts.

During the ride out to Caroline's a million ideas filtered through Jones's mind. More than anything he couldn't believe that in 24 hours so much had changed. At this time the night before he had been drinking a beer with some of his colleagues from the magazine at a bar across the street from the office. Now he was sitting on a train headed toward his girlfriend's place, blind as a bat and unable to read. He had no idea what he would tell her. But more than this uncertainty, he felt bothered by his shame. *That's it,* Jones thought. He felt ashamed to have spent his day playing such an idiotic game reliant on the whims of others. Even worse was the fact that most of the people he had interacted with were people he didn't know, who had no interest in his well-being. Why would they? If he was in their position, say that of his assistant or the ophthalmologist, wouldn't he have behaved similarly? Of course he would have. Jones understood that human beings are naturally selfish, and that this was why people had treated him the way they had that day. And in a way his own selfishness was why he had behaved the way he had as well. *When we have a problem,* Jones thought, *we want an immediate answer, especially when our dilemma is atypical. We want an answer and reassurance that things will be OK. We desire these things even if there is no answer or explanation, even if we realize that it's possible that things will never be OK and return to how they were before. We desire these things because we are human beings and it is in our nature to regard the world from a selfish perspective. But I must resist this temptation and remain calm. I must stop trying to convince myself that I will get out of this and instead just take things as they come. If I am unable to accept the fact that it is possible I might never be able to read again, how will I be able to find a way to continue living?*

These circular questions brought a certain peace to Jones, one that he'd been craving all day. The train ride went by quickly, and before long he realized he was pulling into his girlfriend's stop. He took a deep breath and felt better. *I'll just be straight with Caroline about what's happened,* he thought. Then he stood up and walked to the door to wait for it to open.

*

Outside the subway Jones saw that the sun had set and the sky was already dark. He could see better than before, but he noticed a slight distortion around traffic lights, so he left the disposable sunglasses on. He realized that he probably looked ridiculous, but he didn't care. Jones seriously doubted that he'd bump into anyone important out there. Caroline's neighborhood was basically a war zone. Besides the wine store and a new coffee shop near the subway, the area was filled mostly with liquor stores, bodegas, and check cashing places. Personally he preferred areas that were a bit more developed, but Caroline liked to think of herself as an artistic pioneer.

Fortunately the wine store was just across the street from Caroline's loft. As Jones approached it he saw four tough-looking boys, probably about 16 or 17, hanging out in front of it. They were all drinking out of brown bags. Upon closer inspection the bags appeared to contain bottles of wine. *Strange that they should have such mature tastes,* Jones thought. *But maybe drinking good wine is just the latest fad in these parts?* Jones nodded to the boys as he opened the door.

The store was a typical ritzy wine shop with cedar racks and a few free tasting options at the counter. It was certainly out of place in that neighborhood, but Jones had heard that the owner lived across the street in the same building as his girlfriend and was trying to cultivate the area. *An endeavor that perhaps is working, considering the young clientele drinking outside on the curb,* Jones thought.

Jones walked up to the counter. Hello, said a man standing behind it. Can I help you? Yes, said Jones, I'm looking for some wine. Well you've come to the right place, said the man with a laugh. Yes, I guess I have, said Jones. I'm looking for some specific bottles. He searched through his pockets for the scrap of paper where he'd written down the names of the bottles Caroline wanted. You see I'm not much of a connoisseur myself, Jones continued, but my girlfriend is. I see, said the man. Finally Jones found a piece of paper in his pocket and passed it to the man. Is there any chance you have these two? said Jones. The man picked up the piece of paper and looked at it. Then he put it down on the counter and turned back to Jones. I'm sorry sir, he said, but this seems to be a reminder about an appointment with a neurologist? Oh, said Jones, I'm sorry. He went through his pockets again. Don't worry about it, said the man. You know how it is, said Jones. I always end up stuffing so many things into my pockets. Of course, said the man. I can never find anything, said Jones. He continued searching through his pockets but didn't find any additional scraps of paper. No rush, sir, said the man. Take your time. Maybe I wrote it on the back of my reminder? said Jones. The man flipped over the piece of the paper and looked at it. Yes, he said, this might be it. *What a tricky bastard,* Jones thought. *It's as if he deliberately wants to humiliate me!* Well those are the ones I want, said Jones. But sir, said the man, these names seem incomplete. Excuse me? said Jones. The man pointed to the piece of paper on the counter. Well, all it says is Chateau, said the man. It seems that you've written Chateau twice. Oh no, said Jones. I imagine you're looking for something French, but I have at least three dozen wines with the word Chateau in the name. I see, said Jones. But maybe you'd just like to take a look at the bottles we have? said the man. Maybe seeing the name on the bottle will jog your memory? Sure, said Jones. I could do that, but tonight I don't think I'll find what I'm looking for. I understand, said the man. You do? asked Jones. Of course, said the man. And why is that? asked Jones. Because tonight you won't be able to read the names on the labels, the man continued. How do you know that? said Jones. The man seemed taken aback. He pointed to Jones. When he did, Jones reached up to his face and realized he still had the disposable sunglasses on. I just had my pupils dilated last week, said the man. It was awful. I couldn't see a thing. Tell me about it, said Jones. Maybe just call your girlfriend and ask her? said the man. Hmm, said Jones, I suppose I could.

For a moment Jones thought about just picking out a few bottles himself. But the more he thought about it he realized this was probably a bad idea. He was planning on sharing some serious things with Caroline that night. He wasn't sure if he wanted to risk showing up with something that would offend her refined tastes. If she lives in the neighborhood I may know her, said the man. I go out with Caroline, said Jones. She lives across the street. She's an actress. Of course, said the man. I know Caroline. We're practically neighbors. Then the man pulled out his phone. I'll call her. She's in here all the time. Before Jones had a chance to tell him otherwise the man made the call. Jones listened to his conversation. At first it seemed like the man was making small talk about the neighborhood. Jones thought it was strange that the man hadn't passed him the phone so he could speak to Caroline directly. But the more he thought about it, he reasoned that if it was true that they were friends then this probably wasn't necessary. The conversation did seem to take longer than he thought it would, nearly ten minutes, and this annoyed Jones, but eventually the man walked over to a shelf and picked up two different bottles of wine and brought them to the counter. Then Jones paid for the bottles and was on his way again.

Outside the shop Jones saw that the four kids were still standing on the sidewalk drinking. He nodded to them as he walked away and started across the street, but just as he stepped off the curb he felt someone grab him from behind and push him forward. You better watch yourself, one of the boys yelled after him. Jones didn't fall over, so he just continued walking away from the store as fast as he could and didn't look back until he had crossed the street. The boys were laughing and pointing at him. *Stupid little fuckers,* Jones thought. He felt his pockets. He still had his wallet and phone, but he was missing his keys. *Unbelievable,* Jones thought. *Could those boys have stolen them?*

*

Jones felt relieved as the buzzer sounded and he walked up the stairs to his girlfriend's apartment. Finally he would be able to rest and collect his thoughts. When he got to her floor he found Caroline waiting for him at the door. She wore only her kimono with the interlocking red and gold dragons on it. Her black hair was tied back and still wet from the shower. She looked stunning and greeted Jones with a gentle kiss on his lips as they embraced. What's wrong with your eyes? said Caroline. Oh, these? said Jones. I probably don't need them anymore. He took off the disposable sunglasses and discovered that his eyes were no longer sensitive to light. Did you go to the eye doctor today? asked Caroline. She took the bag containing the wine bottles from Jones and placed it on the counter. I did, he said. Is anything wrong? she asked. Caroline had some sauce cooking on her stove and stepped away to stir it as she spoke. They're not sure, said Jones. The eye doctor dilated my pupils just a month ago. It was the worst, said Caroline. My appointment was in the morning and the rest of the day I couldn't see a thing. Mine was late afternoon, said Jones. Well at least it's dark out now, said Caroline. But there is something that has happened to me I'd like to speak with you about, said Jones. I hope it's nothing serious, said Caroline. Don't tell me those kids outside the wine store hassled you? They actually did, said Jones. I think they may have stolen my keys. That's strange, said Caroline. Tell me about it, said Jones. Well at least you weren't jumped, said Caroline. This is true, said Jones. Then she looked at him. I have some serious news to share with you too, said Caroline. She smiled a little, but then turned back to the sauce. She poured some cream into it and then stirred it. Maybe we should open some of the wine first? said Jones. Of course, said Caroline. She turned away from the sauce and put some noodles into a pot of boiling water.

Then she reduced the heat under the pasta and partially covered the sauce.

Caroline took the wine bottles out of the bag and placed them on the counter. Jones expected her to thank him for picking up the wine she had asked for, but she seemed puzzled and examined each bottle's label closely. Is something wrong? asked Jones. You know, it's no big deal, said Caroline, but you do realize that these aren't the bottles I asked you to buy? What? said Jones. Don't get me wrong, said Caroline, these do look very good. But how can that be? said Jones. After all, you spoke to the owner of the wine shop yourself. I did? said Caroline. Of course you did, said Jones. I couldn't remember the wines you wanted so the man behind the counter offered to call you. He offered to call me? said Caroline. It was strange, said Jones. He said if you lived in the neighborhood he might know you, so I told him that I was with Caroline the actress who lived across the street. Then he pulled out his phone and made a call. Well maybe he confused me with Caroline the artist, she said. Caroline the artist? said Jones. Who's she? One of my downstairs neighbors, said Caroline. I see, said Jones. But why would she tell him what bottles to sell me? Maybe she has her boyfriend coming over tonight and asked him to buy few bottles of wine too? said Caroline. But isn't that just a bit too coincidental, said Jones. Not at all, said Caroline. Today is the first Monday of the month and on the first Monday each woman who lives in my building has her boyfriend over for dinner and asks him to pick up a few bottles of wine on the way over. Are you serious? asked Jones. Of course not, said Caroline. Come on, I'm kidding. That would be absurd. Right, said Jones. You should have just written down the names, silly, she said. She opened one of the bottles and poured each of them a glass. I know I should have, said Jones. Please don't worry about it, said Caroline. Even if you had written down the names you probably would have lost the piece of paper in your pockets. This is true, said Jones. Caroline poured the pasta from the pot into a strainer. Then she took out two bowls and filled each first with pasta and then with a pinkish creamy colored sauce. You mind taking these to the table? she said. Not at all, said Jones. He carried the bowls to the table. Caroline joined him a minute later. She brought the wine.

Jones was still nervous about explaining his illiteracy to her, but the simple act of eating made him feel better. Sitting there eating with Caroline made him realize that he hadn't eaten anything all day. He complimented her on the food and watched as the wine brought color to her pale skin. He found the slight rouge that began to appear on her cheeks irresistible. It almost seemed as if she was glowing. He felt tempted to just take her right there. But there was business to be taken care of first; otherwise he wasn't sure if he'd be able to perform properly. And he'd certainly feel better once he got everything off his chest.

This morning the strangest thing happened to me, said Jones. Really? said Caroline. Yes, said Jones, something potentially serious. It's funny you say that, said Caroline. It is? said Jones. Yes, said Caroline. Because I had a serious thing happen to me this morning too, something extremely serious that will leave a lasting impact on my work. Well me too, said Jones. How strange? It's not strange, said Caroline. It's wonderful! Can I tell you about it dear? She clutched Jones's hand. Or would you rather go first? No, go ahead, said Jones. What happened? Well, said Caroline, it all started with a dream I had last night.

Yes? said Jones. I don't know where I was. I may have been in a cave. It was dark and I know I was all alone, she said. How terrifying, said Jones. It was scary, said Caroline, but what was even worse was that I knew that I was cut off from the rest of the world. Because you were stuck in the cave? said Jones. I guess that's why I felt that way, said Caroline. I just remember feeling this tremendous sense of disconnection. When I woke up I was in a cold sweat. I couldn't get over how that cave is a metaphor for my entire existence. I see, said Jones. But do you? asked Caroline. Her eyes were wide open and she looked more excited than Jones had ever seen her. *I'll have to play my cards right tonight,* he thought. *This has the potential to be a night of wild lovemaking indeed!* Well maybe I don't understand, said Jones. What did the dream mean to you? I interpreted it in terms of my work, said Caroline. I mean in a way being stuck in a cave is like being an actress. Like there I am. I'm just sitting there waiting for someone to give me a call. I'm just waiting for someone to let me out of my cave for a few hours and give me the chance to be great. Some days that happens and other days it doesn't. A lot of waiting is always involved. That makes sense, said Jones. Sure, said Caroline, but that doesn't mean I'm OK with living that way! I mean, who the hell wants to waste their life waiting around in a goddamn cave when there's an entire world out there, a world just waiting to play? That's what the dream made me realize. The dream made me realize that my purpose in life is to play with the world. I want to play with everyone. I want to be constantly making love. I want to be a part of everyone. Hmm, said Jones. How exactly do you plan to go about doing this? By writing a screenplay, silly. Everyone loves the movies. So if I write a movie that every one watches and loves, then I become a part of everything, said Caroline. That's how I walk away from the cave and into the world to play. I see, said Jones. I never really thought about writing before, said Caroline, but then this morning I understood everything. Now I understand why you spend so much time working on your stuff. She moved her hand to Jones's inner thigh. All this time I was jealous of your work and wanted you to give me more attention, but now I realize that you were busy making love to the world too. Well that's certainly one way to put it, said Jones. So as soon as I got out of bed this morning I sat down and started writing a feature. It's about a young hooker who loves what she does because she really likes having sex, but then she meets a guy she really cares about who has a problem with her lifestyle, so she tries to get a respectable job and be good. That sounds like a decent start, said Jones. Do you know how it ends? Of course, said Caroline. She realizes she doesn't fit into the normal world so she goes back to turning tricks. I like that, said Jones. I knew you would, said Caroline. I thought of you this morning when I was brainstorming. I tried my hardest to be cynical! I've taught you well, said Jones. I'm just so excited, said Caroline. Then she jumped up from her seat and ran to her bedroom.

Caroline returned holding a stack of about a dozen pages. She put them down on the table in front of Jones and then sat on his lap. I only finished the first ten pages, she said, but I'm dying to hear what you think. Jones placed his hand around her waist and touched her stomach. He could feel an erection coming on. Of course dear, he said, I'll read them later. Oh, but I can't wait, said Caroline. I read somewhere that the first ten pages are the most important ones. That's true, said Jones. Don't you think you could take a quick look at them now? Jones moved his left hand from her stomach up to her breast and moved his right hand under her robe up her inner thigh. Later, he whispered. He kissed the back of her neck. For a moment he thought things would move forward as he wanted them to, but she shook out of his embrace and slipped off his lap. I'm serious, said Caroline. This is really important to me! I want to hear what you think! Of course dear, said Jones. I understand these things. I would honestly love to look at your work, but right now I physically can't. Caroline took a step back from him. Her face grew confused. What do you mean you physically can't? she said. This is going to sound ridiculous, said Jones. What's your problem? said Caroline. You can't bring yourself to look at the work of a novice like me? Of course not, said Jones. Remember I told you I had something important to talk to you about too? Yes, said Caroline. Well I know this will sounds crazy, said Jones, but I woke up this morning unable to read. What do you mean you woke up unable to read? said Caroline. Are your eyes still messed up from the doctor's? No, said Jones. For some reason I can no longer read letters or numbers. What? said Caroline. You can't be serious? said Caroline. I am, said Jones. But people don't just wake up unable to read, said Caroline. Before today I wouldn't argue with you, said Jones. Did you hit your head or something? said Caroline. No, said Jones. My ophthalmologist couldn't find anything wrong with me, but we'll see what the neurologist thinks tomorrow. You're going to see a neurologist? said Caroline. The ophthalmologist was worried that something might be wrong with my brain, said Jones. What happened exactly? said Caroline. Nothing, really, said Jones. I woke up this morning and felt fine, but then I realized something was wrong when I tried to read the paper on the train. There weren't any words in it. All I could make out were broken lines and ink blobs. Nothing made any sense. Jones grabbed a page of Caroline's screenplay and looked at it. That's how this appears to me too, he said. All I see is a bunch of broken lines and blobs of ink that don't make any sense. Yeah I bet, said Caroline. You're not pulling this shit because you haven't been able to sell your novel? What? said Jones. Are you fucked up? said Caroline. You don't seem drunk, but maybe you're on something. Of course not, said Jones. This just seems pretty bold, said Caroline. What are you talking about? said Jones. Connect the fucking dots, said Caroline. You show up here wearing your eye doctor sunglasses even though it's been dark for hours. Then I tell you I started writing. You try to have sex with me, but when I resist and ask for your opinion of my work, you tell me that you woke up unable to read? Wait just a minute, said Jones. You asshole! said Caroline. If you didn't like my idea, you could have just told me! But I do like your idea, said Jones, especially the solipsistic ending. Then what's going on? said Caroline. I already told you, said Jones. I don't know why, but for some reason today I woke up illiterate. Did something happen at work? asked Caroline. No, said Jones. I wasn't there that long today. After I got in I had my assistant make me an appointment with an ophthalmologist. Then I wrote the final draft of that big review my editor assigned me before I left for the doctor's. You really need to get rid of that slut of an assistant you have, said Caroline. Yes, I know, said Jones. You should have seen the ophthalmologist's office she sent me to. Wait a minute, said Caroline. You wrote the final draft of your review? I know it sounds strange, said Jones, but I'm still able to write. I've been typing and writing so long that hitting the keys and forming letters on the page is an effortless function of habit. Do you really expect me to believe what you're telling me? said Caroline. That's a fair question, said Jones. I know all of this sounds so strange. Are you sure something didn't happen that you're trying to tell me about? said Caroline. Not that I know of, said Jones. And I don't need to remind you that we chose to live this way and that sometimes living the way we have chosen can be difficult, said Caroline. Excuse me? said Jones. The life of the artist, silly, said Caroline.

Then Jones realized Caroline was trying to be tender with him.

I know that you've had a tough time trying to sell your novel, said Caroline, but that's no reason to throw in the towel. I don't intend to, said Jones. Just listen to me, dear, she said. You've always been able to read and you always will be. But you haven't understood a word I've said, Jones protested. Even though it's completely ridiculous, today you say you physically can't read, said Caroline. I find this difficult to believe, but I love you and trust you so I will try my best to believe what you say. At last, said Jones. Thank you! But being the logical individual I am, said Caroline, surely you can understand my refusal to just superficially accept this ailment of yours? Surely you can understand why I wonder about the cause? That seems reasonable enough, said Jones. I'm glad you agree, said Caroline, because in thinking about what has occurred I feel fairly confident that what has happened to you is nothing more than an illusion. But it's not, said Jones. I swear! I think you're so afraid of failure that you've created a condition for yourself as an excuse for your inability to succeed as a writer. That's crazy, said Jones. And while I understand and empathize with your psychological self-defense mechanisms, said Caroline, frankly this pisses me off because it completely fucks up our plan. Our plan? asked Jones. What the hell is wrong with you? Caroline screamed. You knew we had a plan! I'm the actress and you're the writer. We're the quintessential artistic couple. In a way I started the screenplay to be closer to you. I imagined rainy Saturdays spent inside this loft watching you act out the parts I wrote. I imagined lying beside you and giving you my thoughts on your work after being the first to read your manuscript. I imagined all the things we have to look forward to that would only draw us closer. I love who you are and I love what we are. I love what we have the potential to become. Don't you ever think about these things? Of course, said Jones. But really, he was lying. He'd always found it difficult to plan out his life more than a few days ahead of time. But Jones didn't have the heart to confess this to Caroline. I think about you and about us and about how interesting our lives will be in the future, said Caroline. I think about how many friends we'll have and how we will talk about it once we are old and have children, who of course will admire us for providing them with a culturally rich environment to grow up in. I have so many dreams and you're a part of all of them! Now she seemed to be on the verge or tears. I have all these thoughts and then tonight you come over here and tell me you can't read anymore. How am I supposed to interpret that? It feels like you just slammed a door in my face. I'm sorry, Jones started to say, but Caroline stopped him. Listen, she said, I don't really care if you're sorry or not. But everything is on the line tonight. I think you should know that. We always said we were going to take on the world our own way and I think we're doing a damn good job. I always thought you felt the same way, but after what you've said here tonight, I'm not sure I know what you think anymore. So I want to just ask you one thing. Please answer any way you wish. Do you still want what we have? Do you still want to pursue this life with me? Do you still want to chase after our dreams?

After Caroline uttered these words she fell silent. For a moment Jones thought long and hard. More than the magnitude of the questions asked of him, he was shocked that such a pleasant evening had been transformed into a ridiculous discussion just because a few hours before he had woken up unable to read. At first he grew angry with himself and the woman standing before him. *What fucking difference does any of it make?* he thought. Jones was tempted to scream that into her face. But maybe she was right, and the life she had planned would be an enjoyable one. At that moment Jones didn't care either way. He still couldn't get over the fact that this overblown argument had been brought about simply because he'd woken up unable to read.

Jones looked up at Caroline. She seemed to be grinding her teeth. Her face was flushed and her eyes were moist from her tears. Her kimono hung slightly open and he had an excellent view of her beautiful right breast. Despite the absurdity of what had transpired, Jones knew he still wanted her. Standing there before her, he knew he didn't want to hurt her in any way. He knew there was no point in answering her questions truthfully, so instead he asked Caroline to read her screenplay to him. His request caught her off guard, but she obliged. Everything that followed happened just how Jones hoped it would.

CHAPTER 5: THE NEUROLOGIST

When Jones woke up the next morning he lay in bed for a few moments before getting up. He was still at Caroline's place, but she had gone to work. Her loft was silent and Jones found it pleasant to spend a few moments alone with his thoughts before facing the day. He wanted to be ready for whatever lay ahead, though really he wished Caroline was still at home because it would have been nice for him not to have to go to his appointment with the neurologist alone. But he needed to be strong.

Jones reached over to the nightstand for his glasses and put them on. He could still see. His vision seemed the same. Stacked on the nightstand to his side Jones saw some dog-eared paperbacks. Caroline had an insatiable appetite for romance novels. Just for the hell of it he picked one up. On the cover was a half-naked Victorian lady sprawled out on some sort of divan. It was a copy of *120 Days of Sodom*, by Marquis de Sade. Jones wondered if he had given Caroline the book as a present, but he couldn't remember. *Well I suppose I should just be happy she's moved on from Danielle Steel,* he thought. He got out of bed and tossed the book back to the table. Then he froze. *How did I know it was by Marquis de Sade? Is it possible I recognized the cover?* He rushed back toward the table and picked up the book. He saw that he had in fact read the title. Then he flipped it open to a random page and discovered it was true. Once again he was able to read! He was so happy he started to cry. Then he woke up.

*

The sound of someone pounding on his front door pulled Jones out of whatever fantasy sleep had permitted him. After finding his glasses he realized that he was alone in his apartment. The knocking continued for another few minutes, but Jones didn't bother to get up. It was probably his super. Jones worried that he was still angry him. He'd woken him up the night before to get into his apartment because those damn kids outside the wine store stole his keys.

Jones had wanted to stay over at Caroline's place, but he couldn't. After they finished he'd tried to go to sleep, but his mind was too restless. Despite all the things he'd told himself about accepting his fate, he was still nervous about his illiteracy and didn't want his tossing and turning to keep Caroline up all night, so he slipped out once she nodded off.

Eventually the knocking stopped. Jones remained silent. He heard something lightly scraping against the grain of the wood of the door and figured his super was leaning against it, writing him a note. As he waited for the super to leave, Jones reached down the side of his bed and picked up a paperback from the floor. It was a copy of Kafka's *The Trial*. He recognized the cover by sight. *Well, what do I have to lose?* Jones thought. He flipped it open to a random page, but found that the words were just as illegible as they were the day before.

A minute later Jones saw a note appear under his door. Then he heard his super start down the stairs. Jones got out of bed and looked at his clock. Fortunately he owned an older one with hands. It was nearly 10 a.m. He had two hours before his appointment with the neurologist. Jones thought about where he was going and made sure he remembered the address. Then he turned on his laptop and tried to email his editor and his assistant to inform them that he wouldn't be coming into the office that day and would possibly be out for the remainder of the week. From the various screens on his computer Jones was fairly certain that these messages went through, but he couldn't be absolutely sure.

Jones turned on his television. The news was on, so he changed the channel to cartoons and watched them as he ate a light breakfast of coffee and cereal. The story was a simple one, something about a queen bee named Queenie, who didn't want to spend her life reproducing. Instead she wanted to see the world. But the fate of her colony was on the line if she decided to spring free. Jones laughed out loud as he watched. His favorite part was a musical number Queenie did with some grasshoppers that made milk and bits of cereal fly through his nose. *It's really just the simple things that keep us going,* Jones thought as he wiped off his face. Then he showered and shaved, and headed out the door an hour later.

*

The building housing the neurologist's office was one of the most modern-looking structures Jones had ever seen. It was set back from the street on an enormous lot. The exterior was adorned with a number of huge steel pylons that seemed to support an inner web of aluminum and glass. The lobby was completely empty save for a guard station near a bank of elevators in the center.

Can I help you sir? said the guard. Yes, said Jones. I'm here to see the neurologist. And which neurologist would that be? said the guard. I'm not sure, said Jones. This is my first time seeing him. I can't remember his name. Perhaps you'd like to consult the directory? The guard gestured to the wall beside him. Jones assumed it was a list of all the doctors in the building. Is there more than one neurologist working here? asked Jones. Of course, said the guard. Every doctor here is a neurologist. You're kidding, said Jones. Why would I kid you about the neurologists? said the guard. They are very serious men. Yes, said Jones. I suppose they are. Suddenly the name of his doctor came to him. I'm here to see Dr. Pace, said Jones. Ah, Dr. Pace, said the guard. Do you know if he's any good? asked Jones. He's a very fine neurologist indeed, said the guard. Well that's a relief, said Jones. Just take the elevator, said the guard. I've already sent for it. It should let you off on the 26th floor.

Jones stepped into the elevator. As the doors closed, his mind was at ease. *Finally things are working the way they should,* he thought. His journey to the neurologist's had been an anxious one. It felt nice to be where he was and away from the paranoia and fear that had haunted his every move since he left his apartment earlier. It started as he tiptoed down the steps of his building afraid his super would corner him, and continued on the street when a disoriented deliveryman held up a sheet of paper and asked Jones if he knew where the address printed on it was. The crowds on the subway had been miserable; as he crossed the bridge he got pinned to a door by a fat man whose body odor was foul. Though Jones never typically felt claustrophobic on the train, that morning it had gotten to him and he felt on the verge of passing out. Once the train emptied at Canal Street he felt a little better. But then he thought of Floyd the ophthalmologist and wondered if he should have accepted his referral to a neurologist. Perhaps he should have consulted another more reputable ophthalmologist first? He could have at least called around and tried to find a good neurologist himself. But wouldn't that just be putting off the inevitable? Wouldn't it be best just to take his chances with the doctors and reassess his situation after hearing them out? But his life was on the line. Jones's indecision was driving him mad.

When Jones reached the 26th floor the elevator doors opened and he stepped out into one of the largest waiting rooms he had ever seen. Rows of chairs were placed in five parallel rows back to back in a space that seemed to measure at least 30 meters. At the end of the rows there seemed to be a reception window so Jones started walking toward it. The space was sparsely filled with people. Maybe about a fifth of the seats were occupied. Some read magazines and others watched one of the four flat screen televisions that hung in each corner of the room. A few people seemed to be sleeping. Seeing them made Jones concerned. *I hope I'm not stuck waiting here all day*, he thought.

At the reception desk a smiling young woman greeted Jones. She was wearing a pristine white nurse uniform.

Hello Mr. Jones, she said. How are you today? Still feeling illiterate? Jones was stunned. I'm fine, thanks, he said. But I'm a little confused. How did you know about me? How do you know who I am? Please don't be alarmed, said the nurse. Our cameras spotted you in the lobby. Were you looking for me? said Jones. Of course, said the nurse. We look for all our patients the moment they enter the lobby. So do all the other doctors in the building. How does that work exactly? asked Jones. It's really quite a simple process, said the nurse. The cameras scan the face of every person who enters the lobby. Then our computer compares the pictures against the patient files of each doctor in this building. When there is a match, the appropriate doctor's office is notified, just as I was moments ago when you walked into the lobby. You wouldn't believe how much it expedites the check-in process. You've probably noticed that this practice is a strong proponent of technology. I see, said Jones, but how did you know about my condition or have my picture in the first place? I've never been here before. Aren't there some forms you need me to fill out? As far as we're concerned, paper is a thing of the past, said the nurse. We learned of your illiteracy from Dr. Floyd's report. You know, the ophthalmologist? Of course, said Jones. And as for your medical records, said the nurse, they're easily obtainable. So is your picture. I suppose all that makes sense, said Jones. We strive to serve the patient better, said the nurse. Please take a seat. The doctor will see you shortly.

Jones walked back into the waiting room and sat down. Out of habit he reached for a magazine, but then he thought better of it. He gazed across the room at a television. The program seemed to be something about the life cycle of giant squids. Seeing the tentacles made him nauseous, so he turned away. He wanted to watch more cartoons. He thought about walking back up to the reception desk and asking the nurse for the remote so he could change the channel, but in the end decided to stay put. *At a place as advanced as this,* he thought, *the wait can't be long.*

Out of the corner of his eye Jones noticed a man seated slightly to the left across from him. He was wearing a Hawaiian shirt and seemed to be shuffling a deck of cards. But he wasn't paying any attention to what he was doing. His eyes were darting around the top corners of the room where the walls met the ceiling. At first Jones figured the man was trying to watch both of the TVs behind him at the same time. But the man's eyes were moving too fast to pay attention to either program, so Jones assumed he was just nervous. Jones found watching the jittery man entertaining, so he kept looking back at him. At the very least it gave him a way to kill some time. *Such a fragile little fucker,* Jones thought. *But I guess this is to be expected. After all I am at a neurologist's office. I wonder what's wrong with his brain?*

It was only a matter of minutes before Jones found the man staring back at him. Hey, said the man. Yes? said Jones. What are you in for? he asked. Excuse me? said Jones. Who sent you here? said the man. The man was anxious, yet deathly serious. My ophthalmologist, said Jones. Hmm, said the man. So it was your ophthalmologist? Yes, said Jones. That's interesting, said the man. Is it? asked Jones. Yes, said the man. It's the first time I've ever heard of anything like that happening. Really? said Jones. I was under the impression that this sort of thing happened all the time. Well it doesn't, said the man. I'm not sure I follow, said Jones. Whoever said there was anything to follow? said the man. I just find it strange that an eye specialist would send you to get your head checked out. Well if you don't mind me asking, *who* sent you here? said Jones. My shrink, said the man. Oh, said Jones. After months of therapy good old Dr. Bill still couldn't cure me of my gambling addiction so he sent me here to make sure I don't have anything internal going on.

Jones looked back down at the man's hands. He was still playing with the cards. Of course, said Jones. Yeah, I know this is corny and all considering my condition, said the man, but nothing relaxes me quite the same as the feel of a deck of cards. Is something here making you anxious? asked Jones. Well I don't know, said the man sarcastically. Maybe I've just been spending way too much time sitting around in the waiting room of my neurologist? Maybe just sitting here is making me freak out? I'm sorry, said Jones, I didn't mean to be smart. Sorry I snapped, said the man, it's just all these tests. I've come to get some tests done too, said Jones. Well be careful, said the man. Why? said Jones. Because I don't know if you realize it or not, but everything that happens once you walk through the doors of the lobby downstairs is a test. What are you talking about? asked Jones. They have cameras everywhere, said the man. I heard the first thing they do is review the way you interact with the security guard. Then they watch you in the elevator, you know, to see if you pick your nose or not and analyze your body language. Then after you check in, the nurse at the reception desk makes her own assessment of you and files a report. That sounds a bit excessive, said Jones, but I guess it is in their best interest to be thorough in the diagnoses of their patients. They're even watching us talk right now, said the man. Hopefully the fact that we've spoken to one another won't negatively affect the outcome of our individual diagnoses. What do you mean they're watching us now? asked Jones. Take a look for yourself, said the man. He pointed up toward the top of the room where the uppermost edge met the ceiling.

Below the ceiling joint Jones noticed what appeared to be a mirrored panel that ran the complete perimeter of the waiting room. It's like the eye in the sky, said the man. They're probably shitting themselves right now because now they get to watch you react to finding out you're being watched. How strange, said Jones. Some people come here and never actually get to see the doctor, the man continued. Really? said Jones. Yeah, he said. I guess the doctors feel that the best treatment for some patients is just to be watched. After some people check in they're told to take a seat and then after waiting for a few hours they're told that the doctor has been called away to deal with an emergency and that they should come back another day. That's awful, said Jones. The worst part is the same thing happens day after day, said the man. Don't people just get fed up and stop coming to their appointments? said Jones. It's a bit more complicated than that, said the man. What do you mean? asked Jones. Well us human beings are creatures of habit, said the man. Sometimes it's not so easy just to walk away from your routine. That's true, said Jones. Take my own case, said the man. I've been coming here for nearly six months and still haven't seen the doctor. I'm sorry to hear that, said Jones. Yeah, said the man, but they're not. They? asked Jones. The eyes in the sky, said the man. He pointed back to the mirrored strip near the ceiling. Now the doctors can watch you react to the fact that you might be coming back here indefinitely without ever seeing the doctor or receiving a diagnosis. How do you think the doctors are reacting to my reaction? asked Jones. The man looked up to the ceiling, and then turned back to Jones. A large grin appeared on his face. Then he started to laugh.

A door opened into the waiting room and a nurse called Jones's name. At first he thought it was the same nurse who had checked him in, but then he looked over to the reception desk and saw that she was still seated there. *Odd how similar they look,* Jones thought.

*

Jones followed the nurse down a corridor into an examination room. It contained a great deal of machinery, including an MRI scanner. She handed him a hospital gown and instructed him to go into the bathroom and change into it. She also told him to urinate into a cup. When he came out of the bathroom Jones gave her his urine sample. The nurse then checked his vitals and withdrew some blood from his arm. She told Jones that she had to take his fluids to the lab for analysis. A moment after she left a short man walked into the room. He told Jones he was the technician. He instructed Jones to lie down on the platform that slid into one of the large machines. He explained that he was going to give Jones an MRI and that it was extremely important that he remain perfectly still while he was in the machine. Jones complied with the technician's instructions and tried not to think of anything while he lay inside the scanner. After the scan was complete, the platform slid back out of the machine. The technician told Jones that he could change back into his clothes. Is that it? asked Jones after he finished changing in the bathroom. No, said the technician. Now you'll meet with the doctor. I see, said Jones. But what do you think? Excuse me? said the technician. Did anything look abnormal? asked Jones. I'm afraid I'm not permitted to disclose that information, said the technician. Seriously? said Jones. Sir, I could lose my job if I told you anything. The doctor will go over everything with you shortly. Oh, come off it, said Jones. He took a twenty-dollar bill out of his wallet and passed it to the technician. Now why don't you tell me what your fancy little machine says. The technician paused for a moment. He held the bill in his hands and looked back to Jones. Sir, he said, you do realize I'd be taking a substantial risk providing you with this information? Jones passed the technician another twenty. The man stuck the bills into his pocket and opened Jones's file. Oh, he said, so *you're* the illiterate? Yes, said Jones. That's me. What a strange thing to have happen, said the technician. Everyone here can't stop talking about you. Is that right? said Jones. Yeah, said the technician. There's even a bet going around on if you're full of shit or not. That's just great, said Jones. Let's talk about my MRI. Well, I'm sure Dr. Pace will have more to add, said the technician, but as far as I can tell everything looks normal. Jones was relieved to hear this, yet disappointed at the same time. He followed the technician down the corridor. At the end of the hallway the technician showed him into the neurologist's office and told him the doctor would be in to see him shortly.

*

A few minutes later a tall slender man walked into the office. Hello Mr. Jones, said the man, extending his hand. I'm Dr. Pace. Nice to meet you, said Jones. Likewise, said the neurologist. He walked around the desk and took a seat facing Jones. *At last I get to meet the neurologist,* Jones thought, but he accidentally said this out loud. And at last I get to meet the illiterate, said the neurologist with a chuckle. I'm sorry, said Jones. I didn't mean to say that out loud. It's just that since the ophthalmologist didn't find anything wrong with me yesterday I've been eager to meet with you. Don't worry about it, said the neurologist. He picked up a file on his desk and flipped through it. I didn't mean to sound facetious in any way, said Jones. I've found my experience here in your office to be extraordinarily efficient. Well that is our intention, said the neurologist. But tell me, how are you doing? Has anything regarding your condition changed? Not that I have noticed, said Jones. So it's true then, said the neurologist, that right now you are still unable to read letters and numbers. Yes, said Jones. But I'm still able to write. Well that's rational, said the neurologist. It is? asked Jones. Yes, said the neurologist. Similarly, when a person becomes deaf as the result of some unfortunate accident, often they are still able to talk for quite some time. So then my maintaining the ability to write is promising? asked Jones. Well, yes and no, said the neurologist. The problem is, if you don't start reading again soon, eventually you might forget how to write all together. Jesus! said Jones. Yes, said the neurologist. I've read your file. I know you're a professional writer. Obviously this is somewhat serious. Absolutely, said Jones. I don't understand what's going on. Hopefully we can figure that out, said the neurologist. You think so? said Jones. There are no guarantees of course, said the neurologist. But tell me, have you recently experienced any significant changes in your life? Changes? asked Jones. Yes, said the neurologist. You see I want to try to eliminate any significant variables that may or may not have contributed to your condition. I see, said Jones. While we're on the topic of variables, please tell me you don't do drugs any longer? I haven't done any drugs in a while, said Jones. He was surprised by how much the neurologist seemed to know about him and wondered what exactly the ophthalmologist had written in his file. Good, said the neurologist. When I was a young man I snorted my share of cocaine and smoked entire fields of grass. Take it from me, that stuff really messes up your brain. Rehab saved my ass. Otherwise there's no way I would have finished med school. Sir, believe me, said Jones, after what's happened to me I never intend to touch drugs again as long as I live. That a boy, said the neurologist. Now let's get back to your life. Tell me, what's going on? Well, said Jones, not long ago I finished my first novel. Interesting, said the neurologist. Do you view it as a success or a failure? A success, I think, said Jones. Really, said the neurologist, but has it sold? Not yet, said Jones, but I have a good agent. Hmm, said the neurologist, well that's certainly something to consider. It is? asked Jones. Yes, said the neurologist. Have there been any other recent changes? Nothing as significant as the book, said Jones. My girlfriend Caroline and I are getting sort of serious. At least that's what she wants. But you still want to chase tail? asked the neurologist. Not entirely, said Jones, but sort of. It's quite all right, said the neurologist. I've been married 30 years and I've never been able to stop chasing tail. I just can't give it up. Really? said Jones. That's not to say I act on my impulses once I've cornered what I want, said the neurologist. But this thing you're in, this girlfriend of yours, is it a point of stress in your life? Sometimes I guess, said Jones. Interesting, said the neurologist. And I don't suppose she's involved in the arts as well? She's an actress, said Jones. And, well, she just started a screenplay. Which makes her naturally inclined to be attracted to a writer like you? asked the neurologist. I never really thought about it that way, but I guess so, said Jones. And what if you weren't a writer? Do you think that would sour the deal? asked the neurologist. I don't know, said Jones, but you certainly have a point. You think so? asked the neurologist. Yeah, sure, said Jones, I mean if you think so. It's certainly possible, said the neurologist. And that's what you think caused all of this, said Jones. You think my book and my relationship have caused my illiteracy? I have no idea, said the neurologist, but it sort of sounds like self-sabotage. You think I'm doing this to myself? asked Jones. Listen, said the neurologist, I'm not a psychiatrist. I'm only a lowly neurologist. Please understand that analyzing your psychiatric health is not my field of expertise, so I don't know for certain. OK? said Jones. But what I do know is that the most profound moments of my life were the two complete mental breakdowns I suffered. And while I am not overly acquainted with the workings of your mind, it is my personal opinion that you may be approaching one. You think I'm about to have a nervous breakdown? It's nothing to be ashamed of, said the neurologist. My first one hit me when I was only 15. Believe it or not I was an eccentric even back then. I was a recluse, into science and seeing the rest of the world. But my antisocial tendencies didn't keep me from dating the hottest girl at school. We ran in different circles, though, which was always a point of friction. She hung out with the popular crowd and I made my own rules. Eventually the time came to choose what I wanted and I chose myself over her. All her friends went after me. For six months I was constantly harassed and often beaten. But I refused to stand down and I confronted everyone who gave me a hard time head-on. That is, until I collapsed in class one day. That made you have a nervous breakdown? asked Jones. I know it's astonishing, said the neurologist. Even back then, I was an intense young man. It sure sounds like it, said Jones. The second time I cracked I was 25. I was in my third year of med school at the time. I was determined to graduate at the very top of my class. My competitive nature made all my classmates think I was an asshole. My first reaction was indifference, but after a while I realized that I was really fucking over myself. After all, my classmates would be my colleagues one day. Instead of trying to work with them and make the world of medicine better, I was hell-bent on pushing things to the extreme even if that meant destroying that very world. In the end I realized I either had to conform to the standards of my colleagues or drop out of med school. Instead I freaked out. How did things work out in the end? asked Jones. How do you think things worked out? said the neurologist. I got myself a good shrink and started taking a shitload of pills. But what does this have to do with me? said Jones. Do you think my condition is similar to your own? Honestly, I really don't know, said the neurologist. You don't know? asked Jones. No, said the neurologist. I believe what you've told me, but even still, just waking up one morning unable to read is pretty unusual. But what about the tests? asked Jones. I took a look at the pictures from your MRI and as far as I can tell nothing seems to be wrong with you, said the neurologist. That's not to say I don't plan on doing a more in-depth analysis, because I do. Also I want to see what the lab has to say about your fluids. But all that will take a few days.

A few days? said Jones. I can't wait a few days! Well I'm afraid you don't really have a choice, said the neurologist. This entire situation is absurd, said Jones. Sure, said the neurologist, but what isn't these days? True, said Jones. Listen, said the neurologist. I'll give you a call once I get your results back from the lab, but in the meantime try to relax. That's easy for you to say, said Jones. You need to focus on the bright side of things, said the neurologist. There's a bright side? asked Jones. There always is, said the neurologist. It's not every day that you get a chance to reconfigure your life. What's that supposed to mean? asked Jones. Whatever you want it to, said the neurologist. Thanks for your advice, said Jones. You do realize that our bodies have ways of telling us things? said the neurologist. Of course, said Jones. Well, in your case I think that's a good starting point for you, said the neurologist. I think you need to think about what your body is trying to say.

CHAPTER 6: AT HOME

Over the next few days Jones rarely left his apartment. In less than 48 hours his entire world had fallen apart, so after his visit with the neurologist he thought that it would be best for him to take a few days to lie low and think. He sent emails to Caroline, his editor, and his assistant informing them that he had been called out of town to attend a distant relative's funeral and wouldn't be back until the following week. Then he went out and stocked up on whiskey, beer, weed, fresh fruit, and TV dinners. He spent his mornings exercising and eating fruit and his afternoons and evenings lying on his bed watching cartoons. He didn't turn on his computer to check his email and he didn't answer his phone either, though he was sure to always check his voice mail after it rang in case it was the neurologist phoning him with news about his condition.

Days passed without any additional information from the neurologist. The only people who called him were Caroline and his office, but Jones didn't listen to any of the messages they left. At least once a day his super knocked on his door and passed yet another note underneath it. This daily ritual made Jones assume that the man was still angry with him for waking him to get in that night the boys from the wine store stole his keys, but he didn't care what his super or anyone else thought of him. This indifference was new for Jones, and with each day that passed he felt more and more liberated by it. He'd spent his entire life acting in ways he thought would make him look good in the eyes of others and advance his career. Now that his entire life had been called into question, he didn't see reason not to honor each and every selfish whim and behave precisely how he wished. Even still, Jones couldn't help but wonder about the events that had driven him to his current state. *Why have I lived the way I have?* Jones thought. *What meaning have I endeavored to give my life? Why have I always tried to be a writer? Was there any one thing responsible for this impulse?* Only after Jones asked himself these questions did he realize that he had no idea how to answer them. The longer he thought about these things, the more he seemed to lose interest in the entire concept of finding answers: these meditations brought him to the conclusion that he didn't care. Jones was just one man living in an enormous world, and all the things that he had done before discovering his illiteracy mattered just as little as all the things that he would do afterward. *That is the truth,* Jones thought. He found comfort in this realization, but it also saddened him and made him afraid.

Jones felt sure that he still wanted to live, but he didn't know exactly how to go on living. He didn't know what to do now that he was certain that it would be impossible for him to live as he had before. He was still young, just 30 years old, and before discovering his illiteracy had never had any serious medical troubles his entire life. Even when he'd had minor ailments, his natural inclination was always to ignore them and push forward on whatever he was working on at that moment. Jones had always considered doting on things to be irrational and essentially a weakness, so he never permitted himself such lapses in his self-discipline. *Maybe I just push myself forward and resist taking such liberties with my current condition as well?* Jones thought. *Maybe I just need to concentrate on what I am certain of because it is precisely these things that are still under my control. Somehow I have become illiterate. This is my dilemma. So now the task at hand is for me to find a way to remedy this problem, which basically means I need to figure out a way to learn to read.*

Then something occurred to him that he hadn't thought of before. Suppose I try to teach myself? said Jones. But just the thought of doing such a thing made him feel ridiculous. He started to laugh. Could it really be that simple? said Jones. Then he laughed even more. He was talking to himself. It was the first time in his life he had caught himself doing such a thing.

*

The next day Jones set out to teach himself how to read. He wrote out the alphabet letter by letter a number of times to ensure his vision of it was consistent and then transferred each strange character onto a piece of poster board. After he had capital and lowercase versions of all 26 characters, he scanned his bookshelf for something to translate. His eyes stopped on a group of thin paperbacks he believed were his collection of James Bond novels. Jones had never gotten around to reading them. He picked one off the shelf at random. Its cover was bright yellow and filled mostly with text, but there was a small graphic in the middle. A man in a tuxedo, Bond, Jones presumed, was spying on a group of people standing around a roulette wheel. Jones didn't recognize the book. It was perfect. In no time he figured out he was holding *Casino Royale*. Translating words this way was difficult. Lacking the ability to write out the letters he was familiar with, Jones had to rely on his memory letter by letter. But his success was encouraging. Jones flipped open the book. The first word was easy. It was just "The." He could tell after the first two letters and felt no need to compare the third to his chart. The second word was trickier. Jones eventually figured it out, but he had to translate all five letters. They spelled out "scent." It was a frustrating experience, but Jones continued working. After about an hour he had: "The scent and smoke and sweat of a casino are nauseating at three in the morning." *Indeed they are,* Jones thought. For a moment he felt proud of what he had accomplished. But then it occurred to him that the same task would normally take a matter of seconds. This thought depressed him. What was the point of continuing with the next sentence? He rolled a joint and turned on the television instead.

A Road Runner and Wile E. Coyote cartoon was on. It was his favorite. *If only all you needed to communicate in this world was a series of beeps,* Jones thought. But then he thought this was a stupid idea. Eventually he stopped thinking about these things and fell asleep.

*

The following morning Jones woke up to someone pounding on his door. The sound startled him out of a deep slumber. He sat up in bed and put on his glasses. He may have been mistaken, but according to the hands on his clock it seemed to be 7 a.m. Open this goddamn door! a man yelled. Goddammit Jones, the voice continued. If you don't open this door, I'm going to bust it down! Jones recognized the voice. It was his editor. Jones felt his stomach sink. What choice did he have? He got out of bed and opened the door.

The editor walked past Jones into the apartment. He took off his overcoat and threw it down onto Jones's bed. He didn't say hello to Jones or greet him in any way. Then he sat down on the couch. Sir, I can explain, said Jones. But before he had a chance to finish, the editor interrupted him. Do you have any coffee? said the editor. Sure, said Jones. Well why don't you go ahead and make some, the editor continued. Of course, said Jones. He retreated into his kitchen.

Once the coffee was ready Jones poured two cups and carried them out to his living room. He found the editor examining the alphabet chart he had created the day before. Is this why you haven't been coming into work? asked the editor. Felt you had to take a little time off to practice your ABCs? Sir, said Jones, if you just give me a chance, I can explain. Save it, said the editor. I don't have time to waste, so I'll try to keep this brief. Yes? said Jones. That review you turned in to me the other day, said the editor. Listen sir, said Jones, I'm really sorry about that. You see something has happened to me and I haven't felt like myself. Well, good, said the editor. Good? said Jones. If that's the case I hope you never feel normal again, said the editor. Excuse me? said Jones. That was the best goddamn thing you've ever written for the magazine, said the editor. It was? said Jones. By far, said the editor. It was so raw, yet poised. You talk about that book from the point of view of a guy at the end of his rope. Fucking brilliant. Even the masthead is up in arms. What? said Jones. You heard me, said the editor. Really? said Jones. It's fucking good, said the editor. They loved it. You finally cut out all that structural and floral bullshit and just stuck to thinking about each individual word. I don't know what to say, said Jones. Well you can start by explaining where the fuck you've been and why the fuck you haven't been answering your phone or emails. I've been trying to get in touch with you for days. Well like I said, something rather unexpected has happened to me, said Jones. It better be pretty damn serious, said the editor. It's not every day that the masthead takes interest in one of my writers, you know? I realize that, said Jones. I really should have been better about checking my messages. Damn right you should have been, said the editor. Then he paused for a moment and smiled. Wait a minute, so you haven't checked any of them yet? No, said Jones. What happened to me is sort of serious so I've been concentrating all of my attention on my recovery. So you don't know that they want to make you chief book critic and give you a raise? What? said Jones. You blew their socks off and impressed the hell out of me too, said the editor. I see, said Jones. What the fuck do I care if you see or not? said the editor. The question is, do you accept?

Jones wasn't sure what to say to his editor. He'd have to turn the job down. Under normal circumstances he would have eagerly accepted it. But how could he now with his condition? Jones couldn't believe this was happening. That's a very generous offer, said Jones. Damn right it is, said the editor. When I was your age I was still schlepping through gossip copy at the *Post*. It would be a tremendous honor to accept this promotion, said Jones. But, I'm afraid I can't right now. What the hell? said the editor. I can't accept it because of my current condition, said Jones, this thing that just happened to me a few days ago. Which is what exactly? asked the editor. This is going to sound ridiculous, said Jones. Try me, said the editor. Well, a few days ago I woke up unable to read. The editor started laughing. That's good one, he said. I'm not kidding, said Jones. I haven't been to work the past few days because I've been consulting doctors about my condition. Right now I'm waiting to hear back from my neurologist. No one has been able to find anything wrong with me yet, so it's possible it may be serious. Have you lost your mind? asked the editor. What do you mean you can't read anymore? Whenever I look at letters or numbers all I see are strange shapes and broken lines, said Jones. And let me guess, said the editor, this happened right after you turned in that review? No, said Jones, it actually happened the morning I wrote it. I realized something was wrong on my way to work. Then I wrote the review and went to the doctor's. But how were you able to write it if you were unable to read? Because I've been writing and typing for so long, said Jones. My neurologist told me that I might eventually lose these abilities too, but this hasn't happened yet. So what you're saying is that your review was really just something you threw together last minute? Well I did do a substantial amount of work on it the night before, said Jones, but in terms of the actual writing, you're correct. What the hell is wrong with you? said the editor. He stood up and picked up his coat. Excuse me? said Jones. Don't act all clueless and innocent, said the editor. I know exactly what this is. You fucking smart-ass. I know what you really think of the magazine. I know you've always looked down on it. But that's not true at all, protested Jones. Don't bullshit me! said the editor. He was yelling now. I'm not, said Jones. I know there's nothing you want more than to publish that novel of yours, said the editor. Well that is true, said Jones. And I know that to you journalism is just a way of paying your bills, said the editor. Well, sure, said Jones, but I think you misunderstand my position. I respect the magazine and take my job there seriously. I think you misunderstand your own position, said the editor. And I think you're afraid of success. Wake up. Don't you realize that you'd have more influence as a critic and make more money than any of the assholes whose books you review? I don't entirely agree with that, said Jones. Of course you don't, said the editor. Because you're a fucking idealist! Because you want to change the world with your motherfucking poems! There is some truth in what you say, said Jones. But what the fuck? said the editor. Couldn't you have come up with a better excuse? You could have just turned the promotion down or quit your job! Do you really expect me to tell the masthead that the reason you don't want to be chief book critic is because you woke up one morning unable to read? It is a complicated thing to explain, said Jones. What the fuck is that anyway? said the editor. Is that your way of saying fuck off to journalism? I just don't get it. I'm sorry sir, said Jones. I'm still trying to understand these things myself. Perhaps I'll know more once I hear back from my neurologist. And who knows, maybe I'll be cured in a few days and able to accept the promotion after all?

The editor stared at Jones. He looked so angry. You're just such a fucking strange disappointment, he said. Then the editor walked out.

*

Moments later Jones heard more knocking. He jumped up in a rage and pulled open the door. Fuck the editor. He was going to him a piece of his mind. But instead he found his agent, Alicia, standing there. What the hell was that about? she asked. She walked into Jones's apartment. What are you talking about? said Jones. He closed the door behind her. Uh, your editor? said the agent. I've always thought he was a dick, but I just bumped into him on the stairs and he looked crazy. I may have said some things that upset him, said Jones. He told me to talk some sense into you, said the agent. Did he really say that? Yeah, said the agent. He also said you'd lost your mind and something about you waking up unable to read? It's true, said Jones. A few days ago I woke up illiterate. What? said the agent. You can't be serious? When I look at words all I see are broken lines and blobs of ink, said Jones. No one knows what's causing it yet, at least none of the doctors I've seen so far. Well at least you're being proactive about it, said the agent. It's the most insane thing that's ever happened to me, said Jones. I don't know what to do. I think I'm starting to lose it. Well you have had a ton of things going on recently, said the agent. Maybe you just need a break? But I can't stop thinking about it, said Jones. In your position I imagine that would be difficult, said the agent. Tell me about it, said Jones. I tried to call you, said the agent, but apparently you haven't been answering your phone? I'm expecting a call from my neurologist, said Jones. I see, said the agent. Well the thing is nobody wants to buy your novel, and I mean nobody, so I think we should ditch it and you should start writing something else. What? said Jones. It's nothing personal, said the agent, but a lot of the editors I sent it to thought it was too dark to sell. Some even referred to it as sadistic. Everyone agreed that it doesn't really fit into the current marketplace for contemporary fiction. Of course it doesn't, said Jones. I never intended it to fit in with what's out there. It was my intent to create something new. I know, said the agent. But the publishers aren't sure anything else will sell right now and no one is willing to take a risk. I can't believe you're telling me this, said Jones. It's not the end of the world, said the agent. Look at the bright side. I hear you're doing spectacular work for the magazine. Everyone's talking about your review in next month's issue. But how can that be? said Jones. I just turned it in a few days ago. I guess word travels fast, said the agent. One editor who rejected your novel got his hands on it. In his rejection letter he referred to your prose as a reincarnation of the stuff Joan Didion wrote in the '70s. But I don't want to be a reincarnation of Joan Didion, said Jones. I'm not asking you to fall in love with the idea, said the agent, but think about it. Most of the rejection letters I received expressed their admiration for your articles and essays, and asked if you had a nonfiction project in the works. But I don't write nonfiction! said Jones. Sure you do, said the agent. But only to pay my bills, said Jones. Well that may be the case now, said the agent, but I think it's idiotic to be ashamed of something you do well. I hardly gave writing that review any thought at all, said Jones. Do you realize how much the advances are for nonfiction books likely to land on the bestseller list? No, said Jones, but I can imagine. Listen, your novel is good, said the agent. You gave it your best shot and wrote a damn good book. Right now is just a tough market for fiction. I realize this, said Jones. What are you asking me to do? It's your choice, not mine, said the agent. Either keep writing reviews for the magazine in order to support yourself and write fiction when you can, or come up with a decent nonfiction book proposal that would make you enough money to be able to quit your job and do whatever you want. You do realize that in my current condition I am unable to do either of these things? said Jones. Listen, I'm not going to question your condition, said the agent, but if you really want to stop writing journalism, you need a better excuse than illiteracy. But what better excuse could there be? said Jones. I'm not going to argue with you, said the agent, but come on, that's just strange. Isn't it? said Jones. I have to go, said the agent. Let me know how things go with the doctors. The agent stood up and closed the door behind her as she left.

*

Such a strange week this has been, Jones thought. *Such a strange man I have become just because I find myself suddenly unable to read.* But then his reflections were interrupted. Someone was knocking at his door again. *So now Caroline has come to check on me too?* Jones thought. He walked over to the door and opened it. Instead he found his super standing there.

Mr. Jones, I need to have a word with you, said the super. Of course, said Jones. Behind him, Jones heard his phone ring. *What luck!* he thought. We'll have to talk another time, said Jones. I'm expecting a very important phone call. But sir, said the super. I'm sure you can understand, said Jones. He slammed the door in the super's face and ran over to his phone. It was the neurologist. He'd been unable to find anything physically wrong with his brain, but he thought it might be a good idea for Jones to talk to someone. He'd gone ahead and made Jones an appointment with his personal psychiatrist the following day. Jones had never felt more disappointed. I need to see a psychiatrist? asked Jones. Yes, said the neurologist. If you're still feeling illiterate, I think it's for the best. Then the neurologist gave him the address. Jones hung up the phone and wanted to cry, but when he opened his mouth all he managed to do was laugh.

CHAPTER 7: THE PSYCHIATRIST

The next morning Jones set off for the psychiatrist's office. It was located in a neighborhood nearby. Jones got up earlier than he needed to so he would have enough time to walk there from his own apartment. Besides his quick visits to the bodega on his block, it had been more than a week since he had left his place, so it felt good for him to be doing something other than sitting around and watching cartoons. The morning was sunny and the wind felt crisp. Jones treasured every step he took. He didn't even mind that the streets were crowded with commuters. *Off to the rat race,* he thought. *And here I am off to get my head examined.* This made Jones chuckle as he continued up the street.

Being outdoors walking made Jones wonder about his body and physical health. Instead of spending his time trying to understand what had occurred, maybe he should have filled his days with long walks around the city? He resolved to dedicate more time to his physical fitness in the future. Then he tried to stop thinking and just enjoy the peaceful Brooklyn morning. Though he had lost his ability to read, he hadn't lost his ability to enjoy the simple things. Despite what had happened, Jones was still very happy to be alive.

Jones continued to walk and feel better. He watched the row houses in his neighborhood gradually give way to the more gritty area around Atlantic Avenue. After he crossed Atlantic he continued north for another few blocks and eventually he found himself surrounded by brownstones. Before long it seemed that he was getting close to the psychiatrist's office. Just to make sure he was going the right way, Jones stopped another man on the street and asked him if he knew the psychiatrist's address. Just as he'd thought, he was only a block or two away. He followed the man's directions and eventually spotted a white sign hanging outside a brownstone. It was hanging on a post beside the entrance to the ground floor under the steps. Though Jones couldn't read it, he assumed this was the place. Then he looked down at his watch and discovered that he was a half-hour early. Jones didn't want to disturb the psychiatrist before his appointment, so he decided to go buy a cup of coffee and then return to the office. After walking a few blocks and not finding a café or even a deli, he asked a young woman, a student he thought, where he could find coffee and she sent him a few blocks north. The walk was a bit farther away from the psychiatrist's office than he wanted to go, but Jones figured he had plenty of time, so he followed her directions and ended up at an artsy coffee shop a few minutes later.

*

The inside of the coffee shop was a cramped space filled with couches and mismatched furniture. Jones got in line and waited to order. Students crowded every table and

Jones thought he recognized early Bad Religion blaring from the stereo. *Ah, the life of the student,* Jones thought. He'd spent countless hours reading in coffee shops when he'd been in college years before. *Maybe I would have read more back then if I had known that one day I would wake up illiterate?* he thought. Jones looked around the coffee shop to see if he recognized any of the books the students there were reading, but found he didn't recognize a single cover. *Not even one copy of Tropic of Cancer or Slaughterhouse-Five in a student coffee shop? How odd?* He took another look at the books and realized that most of the people there seemed to be reading big art books. The nearby college was an art school, but even still Jones found the absence of paperbacks there odd. He also didn't see a single student working on a computer. *That's strange,* Jones thought. *Here I am in a coffee shop where no one seems to be reading any words?*

When it was his turn to order he couldn't resist asking the woman behind the counter about the absence of books and computers. It's because they're not allowed in here, she said. But why not? said Jones. Because most of us here are artists, so we wanted to create an environment where the music is always loud and people are always talking and the discussion is always about art. I see, said Jones. *Well if my condition doesn't improve,* he thought, *this is just the place for me.* Then he paid for his coffee and headed back to the psychiatrist's office.

*

Outside the shop Jones looked down at his watch and saw that he only had five minutes before his appointment was scheduled to begin. *That line really took forever!* Jones thought. He retraced his steps back toward the psychiatrist's office. Luckily he caught mostly green lights as he walked and seemed to make good time, but when he turned onto the block where he thought the doctor's office was located, it wasn't where he remembered it being before. At first Jones thought that he'd just made a mistake, so he walked down to the next block. But he didn't find the psychiatrist's office there either. Each block of brownstones appeared exactly the same to him and the longer he looked for the office, the more uncertain he became of where he was. And on top of that, now he was late!

Jones spotted a deli in the middle of the block, so he went inside to ask for directions. I'm looking for a psychiatrist's office, said Jones. His name is Dr. Johnson. Maybe you know where I can find him? The man standing behind the counter just stared at Jones. He didn't say a word. At first Jones thought that maybe the proprietor didn't speak English, but then he realized that the man seemed to be shaking his head in disapproval. *Have I done something to make him angry?* Jones wondered. I'm sick of you crazies coming in here, said the man. Excuse me? said Jones. You crazies think that just because I run a deli I know where everything is. Well I've got news for you; this isn't a gas station. I'm sorry to bother you, said Jones, but the thing is I'm running late. Well, whose fault is that? said the man. Mine, of course, said Jones. How far away do you think you are from the doctor's office? I have no idea, said Jones. I'm hardly ever in this neighborhood. So it didn't occur to you to take a look around before you came in here and hassled me? said the man. No, I guess it didn't, said Jones. But the thing is all these brownstones look the same. So you didn't notice that Dr. Johnson's office is next door? said the man. No, said Jones. I'm sorry for wasting your time.

Jones hung his head in shame and walked out of the deli. When he got outside he realized that he was in fact standing outside the psychiatrist's office. He recognized the white sign from before. Jones wondered how he could have missed it. But the important thing was that he was there. He walked to the door below the steps next to the sign and rang the bell. But no one answered. He waited a few minutes. Jones hoped that his tardiness hadn't caused the psychiatrist to go out. He rang the bell again. You're not just crazy, he heard someone say behind him, you're stupid too. He turned around and saw that the man from the deli had come outside to smoke a cigarette. Excuse me? asked Jones. Can't you read? said the man. He pointed to the sign. Huh? said Jones. Dr. Johnson's office, said the man. It's on the top floor. Yes of course, said Jones. He walked up the stairs of the brownstone and hit the buzzer. He heard the lock click, so he pushed open the door and started up the stairs.

*

After climbing up four flights of stairs, Jones came upon a door that was slightly ajar. There was an index card fastened to the outside of it with a pushpin. Jones couldn't read the card, but he figured this must be the psychiatrist's office, so he walked through the doorway. Inside Jones found a sparsely furnished room, which he guessed was the waiting room. Along one wall was a row of folding chairs and in front of them were two upside-down milk crates that served as a coffee table. On top of the crates were a few copies of *National Geographic.* Jones saw two closed doors on the back wall to his right. To his left he saw what appeared to be a kitchen. There was a counter with two stools in front of an opening. Jones noticed an older man with a thick gray goatee seated on the other side of the counter. He was reading a newspaper. As Jones approached him he realized that the man was leaning over a sink.

Dr. Johnson? said Jones. This is his office, said the man. Dr. Johnson, the psychiatrist? said Jones. Yes, said the man. Can I help you? Yes, said Jones. I have an appointment with the doctor, but I'm a little late. Ah, said the man, so you must be the illiterate? Yes, said Jones. At least that seems to be the case. I see, said the man. Don't worry about your tardiness. The doctor has been looking forward to your visit. He has? said Jones. Yes, said the man. He cleared his entire morning schedule so he could have ample time to spend with you. Your condition, this illiteracy of yours—you see, it interests the doctor greatly. Why is that? asked Jones. You'll have to take that up with the doctor, said the man. Come with me. Jones followed the man through one of the doors.

The psychiatrist's office was a stark contrast to the waiting room: A plush carpet covered the floor, and in the back, near the window, was a large oak desk—the doctor's, Jones assumed. One wall had a door that led to the adjoining room. The other walls were lined with bookshelves stacked with books, and in the middle was a long leather couch. Please, have a seat, said the man. He gestured to the couch. The doctor will see you shortly. Then the man walked out of the room and left Jones alone. He was shocked that such a comfortable room, one that seemed so stereotypical of a psychiatrist's office, existed in a place he had assumed was just a regular apartment. *Well, appearances can be deceiving,* Jones thought. He stretched out on the couch. He felt relaxed lying there, waiting for the psychiatrist, and had started drifting off to sleep when he was awoken by the sound of the door.

Jones sat up on the psychiatrist's couch when he saw the door from the adjoining room open. The same man who had shown him into the room minutes earlier appeared again, only now he was wearing a thick button-down cardigan sweater and held a tobacco pipe in his hand. Mr. Jones, said the man, extending his hand. I'm Dr. Johnson. Nice to meet you, said Jones as he shook his hand. The man then took a seat on a chair across from the couch. So I hear you've suddenly become an illiterate, said the psychiatrist. Is that where you'd like to begin?

Wait a second, said Jones. Yes? said the psychiatrist. You just said you're Dr. Johnson, the psychiatrist? said Jones. Yes, of course, said the psychiatrist. But just a moment ago when I asked you if you were Dr. Johnson, you denied it, said Jones. No, said the psychiatrist, I merely informed you that you were in Dr. Johnson's office, which is true. I see, said Jones. Is everything all right? asked the psychiatrist. I guess, said Jones. But then you referred to the doctor and showed me into this room and said the doctor would be in to see me shortly before coming in to see me yourself. Has something I've done offended you? asked the psychiatrist. No, said Jones, but I guess I just assumed you were the doctor's receptionist. That was precisely my intent, said the psychiatrist. Why? asked Jones. Well times are tough, said the psychiatrist, so I had to lay off my receptionist. Oh, said Jones. And you see, experience has taught me that sometimes not being greeted by a receptionist can change the outcome of a patient's session. Lacking a receptionist, some people, especially new patients, think I am an inferior doctor. Really? said Jones. I also find it interesting to initially encounter my patients from this perspective. Some are rude and talk down to me when they think I'm nothing but a lowly receptionist. Others are polite and overly kind. You can't imagine the look on some people's faces when they realize that they've actually been talking to the doctor all along. Especially the rude ones. I know it sounds sadistic, but I really do enjoy seeing them attempt to laugh it all off as a joke while trying to conceal their embarrassment. Well, that certainly is an interesting way to introduce yourself to your patients, said Jones. It never ceases to amaze me how much you can learn about a person based on the way they treat others, said the psychiatrist. I see, said Jones. Did the way I behaved teach you anything about me? Just that you're ashamed of your condition and that it is in your nature to be polite. That's true, said Jones. But many of the people who come to this office are ashamed and polite, the psychiatrist continued, so really your behavior didn't show me anything extraordinary. I guess that's unfortunate then, said Jones. Not really, said the psychiatrist. Typically my initial observations of patients don't end up being important at all; it's more for my own entertainment. Now, let's get started: Why don't you tell me about your problem.

Jones told the psychiatrist about everything that had occurred that week. He spoke fast and went from one thing to the next without stopping, but he was careful to include every last detail. The psychiatrist remained silent as Jones spoke. Besides Jones's voice, the only sound in the room was the light scratching the psychiatrist's pencil made on his pad of paper when he took the occasional note. When Jones finished talking, he felt relieved. It took him nearly fifteen minutes to describe what happened to him and now he was eager to hear what the doctor had to say. But the psychiatrist seemed deeply involved in whatever he was writing. The two men sat in silence for another ten minutes before the psychiatrist finally spoke.

I'm sorry, said the psychiatrist, but I found your story fascinating and it inspired me. I couldn't help myself—I had to write a poem. You wrote a poem? asked Jones. Yes, said the psychiatrist. That's what you've been doing for the past ten minutes we've been sitting here not speaking? said Jones. Yes, said the psychiatrist. You see, writing poems helps me understand myself. I apologize if you think I've been insensitive, but experience has taught me to seize moments of self-examination and inspiration whenever they come; they're not always around when you need them, you know? I suppose that's true, said Jones. And if I am unable to understand myself, how can you expect me to understand you? But aren't you guys already supposed to understand everything? asked Jones. Isn't that what makes you a psychiatrist? Of course, said the psychiatrist. But just because I am gifted at understanding the problems of others doesn't mean I'm any less of a human being. I never said that, said Jones. But you implied it, said the psychiatrist. I'm sorry, said Jones. I didn't mean to criticize you. It's quite all right, said the psychiatrist. It's a common misconception. Despite my professional gifts, I am still a human being who has problems just like you. In fact, if you consider some of *my* problems, you might realize yours are less unique than you perceive them to be. Excuse me? said Jones. You perceive your illiteracy to be a unique issue because the discovery of your condition has caused your world to fall apart, said the psychiatrist. That's right, said Jones. Well, recently I had something similar occur to me, said the psychiatrist. Really? said Jones. I lost everything, said the psychiatrist, and in the end all I had was my mortality. And like you, despite what had occurred I decided that I really did enjoy life and wanted to live. What happened? said Jones. Well, the root of all my problems is really this godforsaken recession we've been stuck in, said the psychiatrist. It's been tough for everybody, said Jones. Yes, said the psychiatrist, especially for those of us in fields deemed not absolutely necessary. I don't follow, said Jones. Son, come on, said the psychiatrist. You're paying me right now to talk about your issues because I have a degree that says I'm really good at making sense of things. I see what you mean, said Jones. Believe it or not, my office hasn't always been in this attic, said the psychiatrist. Oh? said Jones. No, said the psychiatrist. Back before the recession, business was booming. I own this building. My wife and I used to live here in this apartment. Our bedroom used to be in this very room where we now sit. I used to see patients on the ground floor. Well that arrangement certainly makes a little more sense, said Jones. Yes, said the psychiatrist, but then the recession hit and I began to lose patients by the dozens. Eventually I was forced to pack up my office downstairs because the only way for me to pay the mortgage was to rent it out as an apartment. The only logical thing I could do was to move my practice up to my own apartment; this obviously caused some tension between my wife and me. At first it wasn't too bad because she still had a job and was away for most of the day, so she only ever rarely interacted with my patients. But then she lost her job, so I had to lay off my receptionist and give the job to my wife. Things went OK for a while, but I'm sure you can imagine how claustrophobic things get when you and your wife both live and work in the same space. That sounds rough, said Jones. Yes, said the psychiatrist. It was only a matter of time before we both became territorial, roping off corners of the apartment for our exclusive use. Then a general paranoia followed, which prohibited either of us from leaving the apartment for more than an hour or so. We were each nervous that stepping out would allow the other enough time to take over the entire apartment and leave the absent party with no space of their own. But that's ridiculous, said Jones. Desperate times call for desperate measures, said the psychiatrist. That's true, said Jones. What ended up happening? Well, after my wife realized that she wasn't ever going to be able to run me out of the apartment, she began to toy with my psychological health. I began to notice that patients who had always been on time started showing up late. After this continued for a week or two, I realized my wife was to blame. She'd chat and flirt with them when they arrived, and it was only a matter of time before she ran away with one of them. I'm sorry, said Jones. It was a paranoid schizophrenic who also had a chronic masturbating problem, said the psychiatrist. Well, at least she picked a winner, said Jones. It's funny you say that, said the psychiatrist. That's exactly what I told myself to move past it all. Sometimes when I feel lousy I still revisit those thoughts. What do you mean? said Jones. I imagine my ex-wife waking up in the middle of the night to the sound of my ex-patient whacking off. Oh, said Jones. Yes, said the psychiatrist, just the thought of it makes me laugh so hard I cry. But it wasn't always like that. Right after it happened I wanted to die. Really? said Jones. Yes, said the psychiatrist. I couldn't come to terms with the fact that in just six months everything that meant anything to me had become meaningless. I thought about suicide constantly. But in the end I decided I wanted to live, so I accepted my fate and moved on. And how did you do that? asked Jones. Ah, said the psychiatrist, I imagine you only ask me this because you identify with my problems? A little, said Jones. Especially what you said about things becoming meaningless. Yes, of course, said the psychiatrist. I thought you might. It's simple, really. I try to tell as many people as possible about what happened to me. Typically my story makes people feel bad for me, and watching people try to express their pity for me makes me feel good. People are so inarticulate and watching people choke over their words reminds me that despite what has occurred I am still a talented communicator of human emotions. I also write poems about my experience when I feel inspired. It's made all the difference in the world for me. If I didn't inform others about my issues or write about them, my recovery would have been next to impossible. So in a way this appointment is just as much about healing yourself as it is about healing me? asked Jones. It's actually more about my recovery than yours, said the psychiatrist. What? said Jones. How could it not be? said the psychiatrist. If we don't put ourselves first, who will? But what about my illiteracy? said Jones. What about it? said the psychiatrist. I came here under the impression that you'd be able to help me with my condition, said Jones. All my patients do, said the psychiatrist. So do you have anything to say about it? asked Jones. Well I don't know, said the psychiatrist. I've been over your file and there doesn't seem to be anything medically wrong with you, so let's break everything down and see what we have. OK, said Jones. Well, one day you wake up unable to read. Considering your profession, this is a big deal. Not only have you lost your ability to communicate with the rest of the world, but you've also lost your ability to earn a living? Yes, said Jones. Have you ever had a nervous breakdown? said the psychiatrist. I don't think I have, said Jones. Well, well, said the psychiatrist, I'm tempted to say that a nervous breakdown is precisely what is happening to you right now. But I feel fine, said Jones. Yes, said the psychiatrist, but you have chosen a very interesting ailment, one that in a sense justifies some of the decisions you have made that have lead to failure. So you think I'm making this up? asked Jones. I didn't say that, said the psychiatrist. I'm not sure what I believe yet, but I am having trouble believing that everything you've told me is true. And why is that? asked Jones. Because in twenty years of practice I've never met anyone else with a similar condition, said the psychiatrist. People don't just wake up unable to read. Writers don't fall asleep one night and wake up the following morning illiterate. Frankly, I find the possibility to be completely absurd. But I'm not lying, said Jones. I didn't say you were, said the psychiatrist, though you may be unintentionally lying to yourself. Your illiteracy might be some sort of self-defense mechanism, but I'm not sure for what. So you don't think anything is really wrong with me? asked Jones. No, my boy, said the psychiatrist. On the contrary—I find your behavior to be extremely odd, especially your insistence that something has happened to you. Your refusal to accept responsibility is what scares me the most. That and the fact that I am the third or fourth doctor you've seen in a week. But I'm not acting this way deliberately, said Jones. Say whatever you need to, said the psychiatrist, but know that it will be impossible for you to resolve your condition if you are unwilling to acknowledge your faults. But what faults do I need to acknowledge? asked Jones. Well, said the psychiatrist, the answer to that might reside in your failures. What failures? said Jones. For the most part I've led a fairly successful life. I don't question your success, said the psychiatrist. But do you think anything I've told you could be the direct cause of my illiteracy? said Jones. It's possible, but I don't know you all that well, said the psychiatrist. So then what do you propose I do? said Jones. Well, first of all I'd like to see you at least three times a week, said the psychiatrist. That seems like a lot, said Jones. It is, said the psychiatrist, but I need to get to know you, so I need to see you as much as possible. After a few weeks we can probably meet just once a week. I can't promise I'll cure your illiteracy, but I'll certainly try. First I'll need you to tell me everything about yourself. Then I'll need to allow myself an extended period of time to thoroughly digest the things you tell me. So what you're saying is that my recovery will be a long process? said Jones. Of course, said the psychiatrist. You're the first illiterate I've ever attempted to treat. Hopefully I'll learn as much from you as you'll learn from me, but this will take time. So there's nothing I can do to get relief from my condition right away? said Jones. Everyone is always looking for a shortcut, said the psychiatrist. I'm sorry, said Jones. I don't mean to question your methods; it's just that there's nothing I want more than to return to my old life, but that's impossible if I am unable to read. Well, the first thing you need to do is get your priorities straight, said the psychiatrist. Excuse me? said Jones. The logic behind what you just said is entirely flawed, said the psychiatrist. You need to get over your past. It doesn't exist anymore, so stop thinking about it. If you really want to overcome your illiteracy you need to focus on your future. And how do you suggest I do that? said Jones. I'd recommend taking drugs, said the psychiatrist. What sort of drugs? asked Jones. Well, I personally prefer Dexies, said the psychiatrist. Dexies? asked Jones. Yeah, you know, Dexedrine? said the psychiatrist. It's basically prescription speed. And *you* take this? asked Jones. I couldn't live without it, said the psychiatrist. Stimulants keep me thinking forward and don't let me slow down long enough to dwell on my troubles. Do you prescribe this to all your patients? said Jones. Listen, said the psychiatrist, you don't need to pretend you're shocked. I read your file. I know you have a taste for cocaine. Oh, said Jones. The most important thing for you to do right now is to think about the future, said the psychiatrist. I'm not talking about your distant future. Instead of thinking about how much your life has suddenly changed, you need to think about how you want to feel a week from now. Dexedrine will help you to do that. The psychiatrist gave Jones a prescription. Fill this as soon as you can, he said. Trust me, you'll notice a difference by next week. OK, said Jones. Then the psychiatrist looked at his watch. Well, your time is up, he said. I see, said Jones. Come by at the same time tomorrow. I'll plan on it, said Jones. And…relax, the psychiatrist continued. We'll work our way through this. Thanks, said Jones. He stood up and started toward the door. Oh, said the psychiatrist, a regular patient of mine is probably waiting outside. If he is, can you send him in? Sure, said Jones. Then he walked through the door, back into the waiting room.

*

Just as the psychiatrist had suspected, Jones found another patient sitting in the waiting room. Seated on one of the folding chairs was a middle-aged man, somewhat unkempt in appearance with a shaggy blond beard. Your turn, said Jones. The man looked up at him. Are you the illiterate? he said. I am, said Jones. How did you know that? Because I've been eavesdropping on your conversation with the doctor, said the man. I heard everything. Well, that's great, said Jones. Just who the hell do you think you are? I'm a painter, said the man. Well, I didn't mean what I said literally, said Jones. I've had a little experience with illiteracy myself, the painter continued, so I couldn't resist listening to your conversation. What? said Jones. I apologize for eavesdropping, said the painter. But really, I just want to help. You want to help me? asked Jones. Yes, said the painter. You see, I've never lost my ability to read, but one morning, months ago, I woke up unable to paint. You did? asked Jones. Is this still the case? Not entirely, said the painter. Fortunately I've been able to recover some of my abilities and I thought perhaps I might be able to help you recover some of what you've lost as well. But how? asked Jones. Before the painter could answer him, they were interrupted by the psychiatrist. Heinrich? Is that you? Yes, doctor, said the painter. I'll be right in.

Listen, he said, turning to Jones. Come to my place tonight and I'll tell you my story. Can you be there by 7? Sure, said Jones. He never would have thought that after everything he had gone through, he would receive help from this stranger, who really could be just a bum for all he knew. But Jones was desperate, so he agreed to meet the painter later on.

The painter started writing out his address but then stopped. I guess I shouldn't bother writing down my address? he said. No, please do, said Jones. In case I get lost it will be handy to have something to show people on the street. Of course, said the painter. He gave Jones the piece of paper and told him the address. Then the painter walked into the office where the psychiatrist was waiting, and Jones headed out the door.

CHAPTER 8: KILLING TIME

Jones walked out of the psychiatrist's office and looked at his watch. It was only 2 o'clock. That left him with five hours before his meeting with the painter that evening. Every other person he had sought help from since he discovered his condition hadn't delivered, so it was hard for Jones not to have his doubts. For a moment he was temped to run back up the stairs into the psychiatrist's office and demand that the painter tell him what he knew, but in the end he decided against this and figured he'd be better off just killing some time, so he started heading down the street.

The wind was still cold but the sun was stronger now and Jones found it pleasant to be out walking around. After a few blocks he came upon a pharmacy and decided to fill the prescription the psychiatrist had given him. The place was an old mom and pop establishment. The aisles were overfilled with junk and in one corner he noticed a clearance bin of Christmas decorations. He found the pharmacy counter in the back. After waiting a few minutes the pharmacist, an old woman, maybe 70, with long white hair tied back into a bun and wearing a white lab coat, came up to him. He handed her his prescription and noticed she had long red fake fingernails. As she read it she began to frown. She looked up at Jones and shook her head disapprovingly. It'll be ready in an hour, she said. Then she disappeared back behind the counter. *What a cranky old bitch,* Jones thought. On his way out of the store he was tempted to lift something just to stick it to the pharmacist, but decided that if he was going to steal from the pharmacy he should at least wait until they filled his prescription first.

Back out on the street Jones still wasn't sure what he wanted to do so he continued wandering down the block. He thought about calling the magazine and checking in with his assistant, but he remembered how angry his editor had been with him and thought better of the idea. He also thought about calling his girlfriend. Caroline had left him a ton of messages over the past few days and he'd been meaning to get back to her, but he thought it would be better to put off calling her until he had some progress to report. He could tell her about his chance encounter with the painter and his meeting later that night, but he wasn't sure if she'd understand and decided it would be best to call her later after the meeting or the following day. For the time being he needed to focus on himself and avoid all distractions. He just needed to find some place where he could sit and lie low for a few hours. Then he remembered the coffee shop he'd stopped by earlier that forbade books with words. *Perfect,* Jones thought. *That's just the place for me!*

*

The coffee shop was still crowded with students looking at art books. Jones walked in past a few tables toward the counter to make his order. To his surprise the woman working behind it recognized him. Welcome back, she said. Nice to see you. Hi, said Jones. He wasn't sure if he needed to say that it was nice to see her too. It occurred to him that maybe she was just friendly and pretended to recognize everyone who entered the shop. To keep matters simple he just ordered a coffee. So let me guess, once you tasted our brew, you just had to have more? said the woman as she filled a mug for him. Sure, your coffee is great, said Jones, but the thing is a few days ago I woke up illiterate so I think this is just the place for me. For a moment the woman behind the counter looked puzzled. Then she smiled. Whatever man, enjoy it, she said. I definitely will, said Jones. And by the way, the woman continued, I'm Judy. Let me know if you need anything else. Thanks, said Jones. He looked into her eyes and suddenly felt confident that he could fuck this Judy later on if he wanted to. I'm Jones, he said. Then he turned away from her and found a table. Such self-confidence was typically out of character for him, but his thoughts of this possible conquest left him strangely empowered. *How odd?* Jones thought. *Suddenly I feel better than I have all week?*

After he sat down, Jones wasn't sure what to do to pass the time, so he walked over to the window and picked up an art book. Then he walked back to his table and started paging through it. He couldn't read the title, but he was pretty sure the book was about the work of Soutine. He recognized the paintings of raw meat and remembered something someone had told him about the painter's habit of using one individual brush for each color he mixed. He may have been at a dinner party when he heard this. Vaguely he recalled one of his colleagues from the magazine comparing Soutine's technique to Faulkner's original plan to publish *The Sound and the Fury* in colored ink representing the different time periods in the book to make the narratives less confusing for the reader. *An interesting idea,* Jones thought. But at that moment he found that he preferred the simplicity of Soutine. *Am I really losing interest in the written word?* he wondered.

Jones felt at home in the coffee shop. The Dead Kennedys blared from the speakers. "Holiday in Cambodia" had just started. Everyone sitting there just kept talking and arguing. No one was hunched over a tattered journal trying to record their emotions with clunky words. Maybe he would blow off picking up his prescription and his meeting with the painter and instead just sit there until the coffee shop closed, casually flirting with Judy throughout the day. He could wait for her as she locked up and then propose that they go out for dinner. He would seduce her while they ate, and then the two of them would make love later on. The next morning he would go into work with her, and the two of them would make coffee for people side by side throughout the day. Then it would only be a matter of time before Jones's old life faded into oblivion and his new life working at the coffee shop with Judy defined his existence. *Yes,* he thought, *it was possible.* After all, just days before he had woken up unable to read. And now instead of sitting at his desk at the magazine, he was sitting in a coffee shop where books weren't permitted, entertaining sexual fantasies about the barista while waiting for his pills. *How strange,* Jones thought, *how strange my life has become.* What had occurred to him almost didn't seem real. But then he looked around the coffee shop again. There he was, surrounded by art students who refused to read. *Could it be true?* Jones thought. *It was.* He loved being there among other illiterates, not held to task for his condition. For the first time in days he began to feel that he was in control of his life again. Jones even felt free.

Jones heard the door open and he noticed a girl walk into the coffee shop. She had chin-length black hair tucked behind her ears and wore a ridiculously huge pair of sunglasses. Jones noticed that she didn't take them off when she walked inside. *Maybe that's just her style?* he thought. *They do go well with her leather jacket and tight ripped jeans.* Jones felt an erection coming on. He wanted to run to her at once, but instead he gazed back at the images of Soutine. His old life seemed so fast to him, but in this new life it seemed necessary for him to be patient. He examined the pictures of the painting before him and tried his best not to think about the girl. Seconds later he felt someone tap him lightly on the arm. He looked up from his book and saw that it was the girl with the short black hair! Hey, she said, are you into Soutine? Yeah, said Jones. Me too, said the girl. He's my favorite. You mind if I join you? Not at all, said Jones. I'm Veronica, she said. She sat down. I'm Jones, he said. He extended his hand. Do you study painting? she asked. No, said Jones. But you're new at the school, right? said Veronica. No, said Jones. I don't go to art school. Oh? said Veronica. Today is the first time I've ever hung out in this neighborhood and the first time I've been to this coffee shop, said Jones. Isn't it great? said Veronica. Yes, said Jones. I love it. I'm among my own kind here. Your own kind? asked Veronica. About a week ago I woke up illiterate, said Jones, so I feel at home here because books with words are banned and no one reads. You woke up illiterate? said Veronica. Yes, said Jones. I've been seeing a bunch of doctors, but no one knows what's wrong with me. This morning I saw a psychiatrist. His office is just a few blocks away from here. He didn't know what was wrong with me either, but prescribed me some Dexedrine. I'm just killing some time while I wait for my prescription. Veronica looked confused, but then she smiled uneasily. Jones reached out and touched her hand. That's a pretty wild story, she said. Let me guess, you're a writer? I was before I discovered my condition, said Jones. But I guess waking up illiterate sort of fucks that up? Pretty much, said Jones. And you're not bullshitting me? said Veronica. Nope, said Jones. He began to feel her playing with his fingers. That's one of the most far out things I've ever heard, said Veronica. That's how most people react, said Jones. But it's cool your doc gave you Dexies, she continued. I fucking love speed. You can have some if you want, said Jones. That would be killer, said Veronica. If you're around, we should party later. OK, said Jones. Veronica stood up and kissed him on the cheek and whispered the name of the bar where she worked into his ear. She told Jones she had to go, but that he should stop by after 5. Jones watched her walk out the door back onto the street. It occurred to him that she had never taken off her sunglasses as they spoke. He looked at his watch. An hour had passed so he decided that he should go pick up his drugs.

*

The pharmacy was just as empty as it had been when Jones dropped off his prescription earlier. An old man eyed him suspiciously from behind the register when he walked in. He headed to the pharmacy counter in the back. Jones didn't see the old lady so he rang a bell on the counter. A minute or two went by. He still didn't see her, so he rang the bell again. Just one goddamn minute, the old lady yelled. It sounded like she was somewhere in the back where they stored their pills. *What a pain in the ass,* Jones thought. He wished he had filled his prescription at a big chain pharmacy instead. There was still no sign of the old lady, so he picked up a magazine from a nearby rack. He grabbed *The New Yorker,* but put it down when he remembered his condition. He picked up a celebrity gossip magazine and flipped through it. He kept coming across photographs of beautiful people on the beach. Jones loved the beach. For a moment he thought about just dropping everything and going there that instant. But then he saw the old woman approaching the counter from the back. Sorry to disturb you, said Jones. I think my prescription is probably ready. Maybe you remember me? I just dropped it off an hour ago. Sure, said the pharmacist. She passed Jones a bag across the counter. So you're one of that quack Johnson's patients? Excuse me? said Jones. You heard me, said the pharmacist. Well, yes, said Jones. I did see Dr. Johnson this morning. If you see him again and he prescribes you anything, take your business elsewhere, said the pharmacist. Are you serious? said Jones. The old woman pounded her fist on the counter. You're goddamn right I'm serious! If you see that quack again, you tell him I hope he rots in hell! I didn't catch your name, said Jones. He'll know who you're talking about. I've told him not to send you freaks here. I don't have to listen to this, said Jones. He pulled some bills out of his pocket and dropped them on the counter. So get the hell out of here then, said the pharmacist. But know I'm wise to what's going on. I don't know what you're talking about, said Jones. Come on, said the pharmacist. Don't try to play me for a fool. I'm not, said Jones. Today was the first time I visited Dr. Johnson. And do you mind my asking what ailment caused you to visit the good doctor? asked the pharmacist. About a week ago I woke up illiterate, said Jones. Well that's certainly a new one, said the pharmacist, laughing. Did I say something funny? asked Jones. That quack never ceases to amaze me. What are you talking about? asked Jones. Last time I checked the cure for illiteracy isn't trucker speed; it's learning to read. Dr. Johnson dispenses Dexedrine like it's candy. My husband and I own a respectable business here and I won't stand for this shit anymore. But I didn't know, Jones started to say—but he was interrupted. Just get the hell out of here! the pharmacist yelled. And tell that pusher of a doctor you have that his prescriptions won't be filled here anymore!

Jones didn't know what to say back to her, so he figured it was best not to say anything. He had gotten his drugs, so what was the point of fighting with the old pharmacist. He was tempted to try to find out more about Dr. Johnson, but figured that maybe the painter would tell him something later on. He turned away from the old woman and headed out the door.

*

After Jones left the pharmacy he looked at his watch. It was only 4 o'clock. He decided to head over to the bar where Veronica worked early. It was supposed to be just a few blocks away from the pharmacy. In no time Jones seemed to find the place. The bar had no sign or name. People just referred to it as *the bar*. The exterior was just as plain as most dive bars. The walls were painted black and Jones could make out a few neon beer signs through the windows. As he approached Jones spotted a man standing outside the bar smoking. He wore huge sunglasses like the ones Veronica had worn, even though it wasn't sunny out any longer. *Maybe sunglasses are just the in thing at the art college?* Jones thought. He headed through the door.

The place had a bar along the left side of the room. The right side of the room was filled with tables and booths with a pool table in the back. There were about a dozen people inside. It seemed like a lot, considering the early hour. But most of the people there seemed young, so Jones guessed they were students. He walked up to the bar and sat down on a stool. There was an old drunk seated a few stools down from him peering into a glass of whiskey. Jones noticed that the man was wearing sunglasses similar to the ones Veronica had worn earlier too. *That's strange,* he thought. *I guess it's not just the kids?* He looked around the bar at the other patrons and realized that every other person there was wearing sunglasses as well. Not wanting to stick out, Jones found his own sunglasses in his jacket and put them on. Then he signaled to the bartender for a drink.

The bartender seemed to be younger than Jones, but not by much. He wore sunglasses like the rest of the patrons and sported a long braided goatee. *Perhaps he's an ex-student?* Jones thought. Can I help you? said the bartender. Just a beer, please, said Jones. You got it, said the bartender. Jones watched as the bartender poured him a beer and placed it before him. Thanks, said Jones. He put a few dollars on the bar. Listen, said Jones. I have a question for you. Does a girl named Veronica work here? Yeah, said the bartender. She does. Then he lowered his sunglasses and stared at Jones for a few seconds before pushing them back onto the bridge of his nose. So you must be the illiterate? said the bartender. How did you know? said Jones. Settle down sailor, said the bartender. Veronica called and said you'd be coming. She said you'd be bringing a shitload of speed. Oh, right, said Jones. I almost forgot. He pulled the pill bottle out of his pocket and opened it. The doctor advised me to start taking it right away, said Jones. He put a pill in his mouth and swallowed it with a sip of his beer. Perhaps you wouldn't mind if I had one too? asked the bartender. I usually try to stay away from that stuff, but I've been so sluggish today. Last night I hardly slept. And now I'm only in the middle of my shift. Go right ahead, said Jones. He gave the bartender a pill. Just do me a favor and let me know when Veronica gets in? You got it, said the bartender. Then he backed away from Jones and started washing some glasses.

Excuse me sir, Jones heard someone say. He turned toward the voice and realized that the old drunk was speaking to him. Yes? said Jones. I don't mean to intrude or anything, but I couldn't help but notice that you seem to have a bunch of speed. And the thing is, well I've been drinking all day and if I pass out at this bar again, well Tony, he said pointing at the bartender, well he'll throw my ass out on the street. So if it wouldn't be too much trouble? Don't worry about it, said Jones. He passed him a pill. Glad I can help. The man accepted the pill and swallowed it with the rest of the whiskey in his glass. Then he ordered another one for himself and another beer for Jones. Nothing like a little Dexedrine at sunset, said the drunk. How did you know what sort of speed I gave you? said Jones. Son, said the drunk, it's sad, but I know my pills. I see, said Jones. I wasn't always like this, said the drunk. But you know how it is? Sometimes life has its own plans. Of course, said Jones. Life can be hard. Sometimes we're forced to live through difficult things. That's right, said the drunk. Like your condition, for instance? Excuse me? asked Jones. Well I don't mean to be nosy, said the drunk, but I overheard you say you were illiterate? That's correct, said Jones. Well, I'd love to hear your story, said the drunk. You see, long ago a similar thing happened to me. In what way? asked Jones. I used to be a world-renowned philosopher, said the drunk, but obviously some things have changed. What happened? said Jones. Well, one day I woke up unable to think, said the drunk. That's exactly what happened to me, said Jones, only I woke up unable to read. Jones couldn't get over what great luck he seemed to be having and felt more and more confident that before the day was done, he'd meet someone who'd be able to explain his condition to him. He told the drunk about everything that had happened to him over the past week.

Once Jones finished, the drunk chuckled. That's quite a mouthful, he said. Only then did Jones realize how fast he had been talking. *So that must be the Dexedrine?* Jones thought. If it was, Jones decided that he liked popping speed. I made many of the same mistakes you have, said the drunk. Really? said Jones. Yes, said the drunk. The morning I woke up unable to think was one of the scariest things I have ever experienced. Suddenly my brain seemed incapable of forming rational thoughts. I ran to see a bunch of doctors, but no one I saw could figure out what the hell was wrong with me. What did you do? asked

Jones. At first I tried to cure myself, said the drunk. I tried to reacquaint myself with all the logic and philosophy I'd learned over the years. That's funny, said Jones. Just the other day I tried to teach myself how to read. And let me guess, you grew tired of it and quit before you made much progress? Exactly, said Jones. The same thing happened to me, said the drunk. What I didn't realize then was that instead of trying to figure out what had happened to me and find a way back into my old life, I should have tried to meditate on what my new condition meant. I've just started thinking along those lines myself, said Jones. That's good, said the drunk. Any conclusions so far? Not yet, said Jones, besides the fact that most of the doctors I have seen are idiots. Well that's a start, said the drunk. I have a meeting tonight with a painter I met at my psychiatrist's office this morning, said Jones. He said he had experienced something similar and could possibly help. That sounds promising, said the drunk. Often I wonder how many of us have been affected by this illiteracy. So you think there are quite a few of us? asked Jones. Possibly, said the drunk. When did you first discover your condition? said Jones. It's been nearly five years now, said the drunk. Five *years*? said Jones. And you're still unable to think? Yes and no, said the drunk. You see at first I made the same mistakes as you. I invested all my energy in analyzing my condition, which was obviously unproductive given my inability to be rational, and made appointments with dozens of doctors. After a year had passed I realized that while I wasn't getting any better, I also wasn't getting any worse, so I decided that perhaps finding a cure was futile and my energy would be better spent trying to simplify and understand my condition. The more I thought about what had occurred to me, I realized that for whatever reason, whether this was voluntary or involuntary, I'd lost my ability to communicate with the world around me and be successful professionally. While it was my natural assumption that this occurred involuntarily, eventually I forced myself to accept that this was impossible and that I must have been behind it all somehow. People don't just lose their ability to think. I was only 45 years old when this happened to me. I'd never been in better shape my entire life and I just couldn't accept that one night I went to sleep as an intellectual only to wake up mentally retarded! Yes, yes, said Jones. I feel the same way. But the more I thought about it, the more I realized that I've always held a certain amount of contempt for this world. So maybe for whatever reason internally I'd reached my breaking point. Maybe I had to stop lying to myself. Lying? asked Jones. Yes, said the drunk. Because despite everything I've written, I've always known the world is bullshit and so are my contributions to it. What do you mean by that? asked Jones. I might have been OK if I'd been born earlier, in another time, said the drunk, but no one needs philosophy now. So what did you do? said Jones. What did I do? asked the drunk. I guess I just accepted that my body was trying to tell me to stop bullshitting myself and leading a life that was a lie. Yes? asked Jones. Then I sold everything I owned and became the pill-popping drunk you see sitting here today. But are you happier? asked Jones. Am I happier? asked the drunk, chuckling. I can't believe you just asked me that. Am I happier? What do you think? How should I know? said Jones. You shouldn't, said the drunk, but frankly I don't care. You don't care about what? asked Jones. I don't care about happiness, said the drunk. What the fuck does happiness matter if life is shit? That's a good point, said Jones. He turned slightly away from the man. He wasn't sure he wanted to get into the endless sort of discussion the drunk's argument seemed to be leading to, so he looked down at his watch and saw that it was already 6 o'clock. He needed to get going soon if he was going to make it to the painter's on time, so maybe he'd have to just leave some Dexedrine with the bartender for Veronica and stop by the bar and see her another day.

*

Jones stood up and walked toward the back of the bar to use the restroom before he left. As he walked he felt like all the people in the bar were following him with their eyes, but he couldn't be sure because everyone was wearing sunglasses. In the back hallway of the bar Jones found three doors. *That's strange that such a dingy establishment has so many bathrooms,* he thought. He opened the middle door and walked inside, closing it behind him. Inside the room, it was pitch black. Jones couldn't see a thing so he felt along the wall for a light switch. When he found it he flicked it on. To his surprise he found Veronica standing there. She wore a short skirt now instead of her jeans, and was slipping a T-shirt over her head. She was still wearing her sunglasses, even though she had been standing in the dark. Veronica! said Jones. I'm sorry! Jones had never felt more embarrassed. He turned around and started to open the door. Where do you think you're going? asked Veronica. I was looking for the bathroom, but I must have opened the wrong door. Well you'll need to go next door for that, said Veronica.

This is the broom closet. Jones turned back toward her and looked around the room and sure enough she was right. He was standing in the middle of a broom closet. Listen, said Jones, I didn't mean to walk in on you changing. What are you talking about? said Veronica. You were supposed to meet me here an hour ago. Jones was puzzled. I guess I assumed we'd meet at the bar? he said. Well your assumption was incorrect, said Veronica. She moved closer to him. Did you bring the speed? Of course, said Jones. He took out the pill bottle and gave her a handful of Dexedrine. This is amazing, said Veronica. I was starting to get worried. I guess I lost track of time talking to that drunk, said Jones. But now I need to go to see the painter. I'm already running late. Let me at least thank you for these pills before you go, said Veronica. She pinned Jones's back against the wall. Thank me? said Jones. That isn't necessary. What are you talking about? said Veronica. I wanted you the moment I saw you in the coffee shop this morning. And I wanted you too! said Jones. I guess then it's settled, said Veronica. Yes, said Jones. I guess it is settled.

He felt her left hand go down to his crotch and saw her reach behind him with her right. Then the lights went off, and when they were finished he felt spectacular.

*

Jones left Veronica in the broom closet and walked back into the bar. He looked at his watch. It was nearly 6:30 p.m. and the painter's place was a long train ride away. Most likely he'd be late. He was frustrated that he had lost track of time, but then again his experience with

Veronica had rejuvenated him and he'd never felt better. He'd just have to explain all of this to the painter and hope he'd understand. Jones put on his jacket and threw a few dollars on the bar. You were in the bathroom an awful long time, said the bartender. Yes, said Jones, I guess I was. I have a long trip ahead of me, so I needed to use the facilities. I see, said the bartender, but you haven't possibly been raping my employee in the broom closet, have you? What? said Jones. I was only asking, said the bartender. It's just that I haven't seen Veronica yet, and she's never late. How dare you accuse me of rape? said Jones. I wasn't serious, said the bartender. Well, rape is a serious word, said Jones. You should be more careful how you throw it around. And you should be more careful with your interpretation of it, said the drunk. What are you talking about? said Jones. Well, rape is not always a bad thing, said the drunk. I have to go, said Jones. Just consider the metaphoric use of rape in Blake's poetry, the drunk continued. Sometimes absolute conquest is necessary, especially when you're taking a stand against the world. Well, I guess you have a point there, said Jones. He started walking toward the door. Listen friend, said the drunk, you wouldn't happen to have any change you could spare? Can't you see I have to go? Jones yelled. Is everyone here insane? I've already said I'm late! Sorry I bothered you, said the drunk. Then Jones felt ashamed. He realized that the drunk hadn't meant to delay him. And more than that he realized that the drunk was precisely the sort of man he might become if he wasn't able to recover from his condition, so the least he could do was be kind to him. Jones took out his wallet, but he didn't have a single dollar. Then he felt his pockets. He didn't even have any change. He looked back at his wallet.

His credit cards caught his eye, so he picked one out and gave it to the drunk. I don't have any money, said Jones, but why don't you take this? Go on a bender for all I care. I won't report it stolen until the day after tomorrow. I promise. The drunk seemed shocked. Uh, thanks, said the drunk. He accepted the card suspiciously and turned back to his drink.

Jones turned away from him and started walking. Behind him he heard laughter, but Jones didn't have time to find out if he was the cause of this laughter or not. He was running late for a meeting that might change his life, so Jones ignored everything and rushed out the door.

CHAPTER 9: THE PAINTER AND THE CAPITALIST

It took forever, but finally Jones arrived in the painter's neighborhood. He was already an hour late, so he hurried down the subway stairs from the elevated platform onto the street toward the painter's place. It was a gritty section of Brooklyn. Most of the buildings around the subway stop looked abandoned. Jones walked block after block without seeing a single bodega. He spotted a few small fires burning in trash cans in some of the alleys between the buildings. Jones could make out faint traces of silhouettes standing around the flames. But that was the only sign people lived there. Otherwise the neighborhood looked like a war zone.

When Jones reached the address the painter had given him, he found himself standing outside the corrugated steel roll-down door of what appeared to be a warehouse. *So this is where the painter has ended up after his recovery?* Jones wondered. He wasn't positive that he had remembered the correct address and wished he'd asked the painter for his phone number too, but Jones figured he didn't have anything to lose and pounded on the door.

The reverberations of the metal echoed loudly into the empty street and caused some dogs to start barking. Jones turned around and looked for them. The barking seemed to be coming from a junkyard across the street. *Just great,* Jones thought. *What a headache.* After a few minutes passed without anyone coming to the door, Jones pounded on it again. The sound made the dogs bark and Jones wondered if he'd been set up. *Perhaps this is all some sort of joke,* he thought. *Maybe the psychiatrist is behind it? Could this be a way for him to trick me into abandoning my former life through forcing me to encounter psychological ridicule and physical danger?*

Jones pounded harder and the dogs barked at him again. Jones was livid. He found a chunk of concrete lying on the sidewalk and hurled it across the street into the junkyard. But the barking continued. He hurled another piece of concrete, and then another after that. If this is what I've been reduced to, so be it! Jones screamed out into the empty street. Here I am in the middle of nowhere trying to kill some junkyard dogs? Well fine, Jones continued. I'll stay here all night if I have to! I'll stay until I make my first kill!

Jones picked up another chunk of concrete, but just as he was about to throw it a bright light shined on him. Then he heard someone cock a gun. You hold it right there, a hoarse voice called out. Jones froze and dropped the chunk of concrete. He looked toward where the voice had come from, but all he could make out was a burning ember. He guessed it was the man's cigar. What's the idea trying to kill my dogs? said the man. How would you like it if I kill you tonight, crackhead? I'm sorry, said Jones. He tried to shield his eyes from the light. Shut up! yelled the man. But I can explain, said Jones. A gunshot went off. Jones's stomach sank. Then he realized the man had shot into the air. You think I'm kidding? said the man.

No, said Jones. Good, said the man. Now put your hands up and don't move. Jones did as he was told. Look, said Jones, I'm sorry if I've harmed your dogs. I didn't mean to. I'm running extremely late to an important meeting. It's with a painter who lives nearby. Maybe you know him? The man paused for a second. You know Heinrich? he said. Yes, said Jones. I'll pay for any damages I've caused. I think we've had a misunderstanding. How exactly do you know Heinrich? asked the man. Well if you must know, said Jones, we met this morning at a psychiatrist's office. At a psychiatrist's? asked the man. Yes, said Jones. Apparently the painter and I use the same shrink. Oh, said the man with a chuckle. He lowered his gun and moved the light away from Jones's eyes. So you must be the illiterate? Yes, said Jones. Well, why didn't you say so? said the man. Heinrich mentioned you'd be coming by. Have I caused any damage to your dogs? asked Jones. Let's have a look, said the man. Jones watched as the man walked down some metal stairs. He shined his light on his dogs and then around the junkyard. No, said the man. In a way it's good for the dogs to get attacked every now and then. It keeps up their reflexes. I'm really sorry for throwing that concrete, said Jones. I shouldn't have. I've had a strange day and when I got out here no one replied to my knocks at the painter's door except your dogs so I guess I just lost my temper. I understand, said the man. He reached into one of his pockets and turned to his dogs. He threw a handful of something out to them and Jones watched the animals eat whatever the man had thrown. Then he looked back at Jones. Can I ask you something? said the man. Sure, said Jones. Just how did you expect to get any response banging on that door? said the man. Excuse me? said Jones. That door goes to the loading dock of the painter's warehouse, said the man. It's possible the capitalist might be in the back mixing paint, but it's also possible no one's out there right now because it's late. The capitalist? said Jones. But doesn't the painter live here? Yes, said the man, but he's only rarely in the warehouse. Didn't you notice the other door? There's another door? said Jones. The man shined his light to the left of where Jones was standing onto a regular sized door next to the one Jones had been pounding on. Jones noticed a doorbell next to it. Was it possible that he had walked right by it and not seen it? Jones had no idea. In the future he'd have to be more careful. A moment before he had almost been shot! Thanks, said Jones. Sorry to have bothered you. Don't worry about it, said the man. Then Jones turned back to the door and rang the bell.

*

Moments later a short chubby man opened the door. He was going bald on the top of his head and wore a tiny pair of gold spectacles perched at the end of his nose. At first Jones thought the man looked like a banker and must be the capitalist the man in the junkyard had mentioned, but then he noticed he was wearing a pair of paint-speckled coveralls and figured that maybe this was the painter's assistant. Yes? said the short man. I've come to see the painter, said Jones. Oh, said the short man, so you must be the illiterate? Yes, said Jones. That's me. Well, come in, said the short man. Heinrich has been expecting you.

Jones followed the short man down a long hallway. The walls were made of cinder blocks and at the end of it were two doors. The short man opened the one on the right and Jones followed him, but then the short man turned around and stopped him. Heinrich is waiting for you in his office, he said. It's just through the other door. What's in there? said Jones. He pointed to the door the man was about to enter. Why it's our warehouse, he said. Your warehouse? said Jones. Yes, said the short man. It's where we keep the paint. Take a look if you like. The short man stepped aside and Jones peered around the corner. He saw at least a dozen rows of large steel racks. Most held wooden pallets stacked high with five-gallon buckets of paint. That's quite a lot of paint, said Jones. Yes, said the short man. If you'll excuse me, I have some mixing to do. Mixing? said Jones. So you're working inside the warehouse right now? Yes, said the short man. Were you working inside the warehouse just a minute ago? said Jones. I've been mixing paint all night, said the short man. You have? said Jones. Tell me then, did you hear me just moments ago when I was pounding on the door? Of course, said the short man. You were pounding quite loudly. It would have been impossible not to hear. Why didn't you let me in? said Jones. Because you were pounding on the wrong door, said the short man. What difference does it make? said Jones. All the difference in the world, said the short man. But that's absurd, said Jones. Hardly, said the short man. For one thing, it's cold out tonight and if I had opened the warehouse door all the heat would have escaped. I have at least four or five hours of mixing to complete tonight. Without heat I assure you that task would be extremely unpleasant. Then there is the fact that I was the only one who heard your pounding. You see, from his office the painter can't hear when people knock on the loading dock door, but he can hear the doorbell. When I heard the pounding I was in the middle of something. You can't just expect me to stop whatever I'm doing to respond to pounding. But if you had rung the bell at the correct door, eventually the painter would have answered it. But didn't you say you were expecting me? said Jones. Yes, said the short man. But how was I supposed to know that it was you pounding on the door? You'd be surprised how much pounding we get around here. It seems people are naturally attracted to pounding on corrugated steel doors. But your neighbor just pulled a gun on me! said Jones. If you had just answered the door I could have avoided that! Well you have no one to blame for that predicament but yourself, said the short man. I guess you're right about that, said Jones. Yes, I suppose I am, said the short man. Then he walked back into the warehouse. Jones turned to the other door and knocked. Come in, said the painter. Then Jones walked into the painter's office.

*

The painter was seated behind a large mahogany desk that stretched nearly the entire length of the room. In front of the desk were two Chippendale chairs. The painter gestured for Jones to take a seat, so he sat down and looked around the rest of the office. On the floor was an antique-looking Oriental rug and on the walls hung portraits of great businessmen. Jones recognized J.P. Morgan and Cornelius Vanderbilt, but was at a loss to name the others. Under the portraits was a small bar, where there was a row of crystal glasses. On the back wall was a huge floor-to-ceiling bookcase, containing hundreds of books. *What a classy spot,* Jones thought.

Welcome, said the painter. I'm so glad you could come. He extended his hand. He still looked just as disheveled as he had before, but now he wore a red silk smoking jacket over his clothes. Hello, said Jones. Thanks for having me. Care for anything to drink? asked the painter. Sure, said Jones. Excellent, said the painter. He stood up and walked to the bar. My partner only ever rarely drinks these days, so it's nice to have some company. Is your partner the short chubby man who answered the door? said Jones. Yes, said the painter. He handed Jones a large glass of Scotch. Hopefully he wasn't rude? Not at all, said Jones. That's good, said the painter. It's hard to ever know how the capitalist will react to strangers. So that's the capitalist? said Jones. He took a sip of his drink. Yes, said the painter. He's a brilliant man, but a tad socially awkward. I see, said Jones. I trust you found the place all right? asked the painter. He sat back down in his chair behind the desk. Yes, said Jones, only at first I was confused to find a warehouse here. Were you? asked the painter. But how else could I run my business? I did tell you earlier that I was a painter? Yes, said Jones, but I guess I assumed you were an artist. I had no idea you sold paint. Can't a man do both? asked the painter. Well I suppose you could, said Jones. *This painter is a tricky one,* Jones thought. He worried that already he had begun to make a poor impression on the man. Relax, said the painter. I don't mean to make you nervous. Your error is quite a common mistake. It is? said Jones. Yes, said the painter, especially since I used to be an artist. You were? said Jones. Well it would be more accurate to say I was an artistic painter. That's what I thought you meant when you mentioned your own illiteracy to me at the psychiatrist's office, said Jones. I thought you meant that you'd lost your ability to create art? Well I did, said the painter. This business of selling paint is relatively new to me, but it has been a crucial part of *my cure.* Your cure? asked Jones. Yes, said the painter, the cure to my own illiteracy. *Finally an illiterate who had found a cure!* Jones thought. He was ecstatic. What cured you? asked Jones. Was it the psychiatrist? No, said the painter. I only continue seeing him because the bastard got me hooked on Dexedrine and now I can't function without it. He prescribed that to me too, said Jones. Really? said the painter. You wouldn't happen to have any on you? I actually do, said Jones. Any chance you can spare a few? said the painter. I hate to ask, but the thing is I'm running a little low. Don't worry about it, said Jones. He tossed his pill bottle to the painter. Take as many as you want. Will you tell me how you found a cure for your illiteracy? Of course, said the painter. He popped a few pills. That's why I invited you out here tonight. But first why don't you tell me a little more about your condition. What do you want to know? said Jones. When I arrived at the psychiatrist's office your session was already underway, so I only really heard half of your story, said the painter. But from what I understand, one morning about a week ago you woke up unable to read? Yes, said Jones. Well why don't you tell me about everything that has occurred since you discovered your condition up until you arrived here in my office tonight? said the painter. OK, said Jones. And then he told the painter everything.

*

You've told me quite an interesting story, said the painter once Jones finished. You've told me something that rings close to home and reminds me of the sort of man I once was. Really? said Jones. Absolutely, said the painter. I feel fairly confident I can help you. You do? asked Jones. Yes, said the painter. Not long ago I was just like you. I was a struggling artist living here in this great city. My specialty was mixed media. I liked to create enormous collages on plywood with oil paint, India ink, and newspaper. But you know how it is. I was forced to take on other projects to pay my bills. Sometimes I got freelance illustration work and other times I got stuck teaching art at a community college. I hated the outside work, but it allowed me to pursue my passion so I accepted it. I accepted the sacrifices I had to make because I believed in myself. After a while these sacrifices seemed to pay off. I'd accumulated a large body of work and started visiting the galleries with my slides. Eventually I was offered a prominent place in a group show featuring emerging artists. I couldn't have hoped for anything more. I went out the night I found out and partied until dawn. God, how I loved my life that night! When I woke up the following afternoon I had a massive hangover, but I ignored my headache and started setting up my materials to work. This was the first day of my new life, so I wanted to start it right. I started squirting out tubes of paint and mixing them to find just the right shade for an abstract image I'd been dreaming about. I added colors as impulsively as I always did. A little cadmium yellow here, a little forest green there: a little white, a little black, a little brown, a little blue. Then I started drawing shapes with my brush and applying the paint to the plywood I had prepared. But after I finished all I saw was a hideous washed-out shade of gray. I wiped the wood clean and remixed my paint. Then I tried again, but I got the same ugly color as before. This made me assume that my hangover must have been affecting me more than I'd thought, so I put away my things and went back to bed. The next day I tried to paint again but encountered the same results. I tried to paint the day after that and the next day too, but nothing changed. Somehow I'd lost my ability to properly perceive colors and was therefore unable to mix paint. When I realized this I was crushed and confused, but more than anything I was afraid. My initial reaction was similar to your own. I sought help from doctors. At first I had the notion that somehow I'd gone color-blind. I made appointments with any doctor who would see me. But no one could find anything wrong with my eyes or my mind. Weeks passed and the gallery where I was supposed to show my work grew impatient because I didn't have anything to give them. I lost my life that day and I lost my ability to make money. I lost my entire identity, everything that I had worked toward for over 35 years. One day I was an emerging artist and the next day I was a lunatic. I know what you mean! said Jones. I feel the same way. What did you do? Well, I followed the advice of my doctors for about a year, said the painter, but my condition didn't improve, so eventually I decided to take matters into my own hands. Your own hands? said Jones. Yes, said the painter. I stopped going to see my doctors and I sold everything I owned. Then I moved into this building. It was abandoned at the time so I broke in and started squatting here. I began to spend my days reading at the library and my nights meditating about who I really was. I contemplated a multitude of things including the aesthetic nature of art. I especially thought about the lives of the successful artists who I admired and wondered if I had ever really had the talent and drive to be one of them. You see my idea was that despite my minimal success, perhaps I had embarked down an incorrect career path. Maybe I wasn't meant to be an artist? Maybe my entire life had been a waste of time and my body was just trying to point this out to me before it was too late? Did you figure anything out? asked Jones. Yes, said the painter. In the end I concluded that I was never meant to be an artist at all. Really? said Jones. Yes, said the painter, but I reached that conclusion only after I encountered a peculiar idea. You see, I came across it one day when I was reading. It's funny, but I found the answer to all my problems and the cure to my condition when I stumbled upon this remarkable book. You found your cure in a book? asked Jones. Yes, said the painter. It was almost as if it was waiting for me. In those days I read everything from books on Buddhist meditation to biographies and fiction. One day I happened to pick up this enormous novel by the Chilean novelist Roberto Bolaño called *2666*. Bolaño? said Jones. I don't think I've heard of him. It was a whale of a book, said the painter. Its size delighted me because reading it would take up days of my time. I see, said Jones. In the first section I came across the story of an English painter. He's not a main character and I forget his name. But because he was a painter, I noticed him. Of course, said Jones. One day he decides to cut off his painting hand. He decides to mutilate himself? asked Jones. Yes, said the painter. Then he mummifies his severed hand and affixes it to a self-portrait he's been working on for an upcoming show. Really? said Jones. Yeah, said the painter. The self-portrait becomes the crowning achievement of the show, a masterpiece, so to speak, and causes the painter to be regarded as the star artist of his generation. But how is the painter after cutting off his hand? said Jones. Does anything happen to him? After the show he's hospitalized in a sanitarium in another country, said the painter. It's in Switzerland, I think? Because naturally you'd have to be crazy to cut off your hand if you were an artist on the verge of success, said Jones. That's a point of debate between the four characters in the first section of the novel, said the painter. Eventually one of the characters has the opportunity to ask the handless painter why he mutilated himself. Do you have any idea what the painter tells him? Maybe because he had to, said Jones. Like maybe for whatever reason he thought that at that moment in time his career as an artist was over, so he felt that he needed to make a symbolic gesture to signify this? Not at all, said the painter. He cut off his hand for the money. For the money? asked Jones. Did someone pay him for his hand? Not exactly, said the painter. Someone bought the painting featuring it of course. But he cut off his hand because in doing so he knew that he would be ensuring his value in the art world. And he was right. It's true he would never be able to paint well again, but it's also true that he'd never have to work another day of his life. And most importantly his legacy was sealed. People do not look to art just to find beauty and inspiration. People look to art to find stories of endurance and mythological achievement. People thirst for artists whose messy lives spill into their work and tell tales of struggle and survival. People look to the arts to give them a reason to go on. If the artist isn't willing to mutilate himself, he should find a new line of work!

I know these aren't easy things to hear, the painter continued, but you should be thankful for this wake-up call. I certainly was. Look to the bright side of things. If in the light of all this you still think you're the writer you thought you were, write the novel you think will change the world and work so hard on it you drive yourself crazy. But, if you realize that you're not willing to die for your art, I'd suggest that you listen to what your body is trying to tell you. Perhaps the time has come for you to grow up and figure out something else to do. That's what I discovered. I wasn't like the great artists who I revered. I wasn't willing to mutilate myself to create a picture that would ensure my eventual fame. Maybe I didn't have the stomach for that sort of thing. Then again maybe I wasn't crazy enough. My point is that after contemplating my own illiteracy I realized that I had to find a different way to live and the day I decided to pursue this path was the happiest day of my life. What did you decide to do? asked Jones. Fortunately I had the good luck to meet my friend Ludwig. He was a capitalist, said the painter. A capitalist? said Jones. Yes, said the painter, standing up. I want to show you something. Then Jones followed him out the door.

*

Jones and the painter walked into the warehouse. They found the capitalist standing above a large contraption that seemed to contain a vat of paint. This, my friend, is the foundation of my business, said the painter. Housed here in this warehouse are over 500 different kinds of interior and exterior paint, some of which is custom-made right here by my friend Ludwig. *But I thought you were the painter and he was the capitalist?* Jones thought, but he kept his confusion to himself. About halfway into the room the painter stopped and faced him.

After I realized I wasn't cut out to be an artist I grew depressed, the painter continued. It even became difficult for me to find comfort in books. And on top of that I was hardly eating. Suicide was a daily consideration. Then one day I just threw my hands up in the air and decided to go out in a blaze of glory. My plan was to rob a bank. If the police showed up, I'd pretend I had a gun and provoke them into shooting me dead. If I succeeded, I'd take all the money I could and run away somewhere to start over. On the appointed day I made all the necessary preparations and went to the bank, but when I walked inside the lobby I realized I couldn't go through with it. Just the thought of threatening another human being made me sick to my stomach. I searched for a bathroom where I could puke, but instead I found a stairwell. After vomiting on the floor I started climbing the stairs. I didn't really have anything I was supposed to be doing that day because I cleared my schedule for the robbery, so I guess my instinct to climb the stairs was natural enough. Next thing I knew, there I was standing on the roof. It occurred to me that the building the bank was in was fairly high and that falling from the top would definitely be fatal, so then I decided to jump. Fate had led me to the roof so my decision was a simple one. I headed toward the ledge ready to die. But then I bumped into Ludwig.

Do you remember how white I looked? said the painter. I do, said the capitalist, looking up from his paint. And do you remember how desperate I was? Of course, said the painter. You were seated on the edge of the building lifting yourself up and down with your arms. I think I was trying to exhaust myself and cause my arms to give out so my fall would be somewhat accidental, said the capitalist. At the time Ludwig was a powerful capitalist, said the painter. He handled major investments for the bank below. Yes, said the capitalist. My grandfather founded that bank. Finance was our family business. But one morning Ludwig woke up and experienced a form of illiteracy too, said the painter. It was the strangest thing, said the capitalist, but I guess I always sort of saw it coming. I never liked what I did, but that didn't mean I wasn't good at it. I made my first million by the time I was 25. If I played my cards right I would've had an extremely lucrative career. But one morning I woke up unable to compute basic financial figures. Really? said Jones. Yes, said the capitalist. At first I just thought I was ill, but all the doctors I saw said there was nothing wrong with me so I went back to work. A month later I had lost millions of my clients' money and was being investigated for fraud. Now don't get me wrong, the capitalist continued, I had enough money put away to live off for the rest of my life, but I couldn't deal with the shame of my sudden failures. Colleagues who I thought of as friends laughed at me behind my back and no one would associate with me. After a while I'd had enough, so I wrote out a will donating all my money to charity and then climbed up to the roof, where I bumped into Heinrich right before I was about to take the plunge. You should have seen how surprised he looked when he saw me, said the painter. I think he actually yelled at me at first. I think you told me I had some nerve interrupting you. I believe you're correct, said the capitalist with a chuckle. And then you told me that you had just as much of a right to be up on the roof as I did. And you agreed with me, said the painter. I did, said the capitalist. Then I demanded that you tell me what had driven you over the edge. You see, said the painter to Jones, this was the start of our partnership. I'm not sure I follow, said Jones. It's simple really, said the capitalist. Heinrich told me that he was an artist who found it impossible to paint anymore. And Ludwig told me that he was a capitalist who found it impossible to make informed investments any longer, said the painter. At first we commiserated with each other. I had a bottle with me on to the roof, said the capitalist. It was good stuff, right? asked the painter. Yes, said the capitalist, a very rare Scotch. We sat there on the roof all day getting ridiculously drunk, said the painter. And at some point I happened to mention how absurd it was that I'd spent my entire life saving money only to end up giving it all away, said the capitalist. And I happened to mention how much I hated charities, said the painter. And I remember this made me chuckle, said the capitalist, because I'd always found their business practices to be shameful. And then I pointed out that there we were about to throw ourselves off a skyscraper, said the painter, but somewhere there was some idealist schmuck who stood to grow absurdly rich. You see, said the capitalist, I had enough saved to fuel a charity's operational budget for decades. And at the very thought of that both of us started rolling around laughing, said the painter. Before that moment I hadn't laughed in weeks, said the capitalist. Neither had I, said the painter. And by god it felt good to laugh! said the capitalist. It really did, said the painter. Standing there that evening it was almost as if we were laughing at the stupidity of the entire world. So then we made a pact that no matter what happened we wouldn't waste any of my money on philanthropy, said the capitalist. And then, said the painter, we made a plan.

Our first decision was that we would use my money to create new lives for ourselves, said the capitalist. We began to talk about what these new lives might be, said the painter. It dawned on me that both of us had sets of skills that had led us to success in our individual lives, said the capitalist. The problem, though, was that we could no longer use these skills ourselves. Then I said that maybe we could teach these skills to each other, said the painter. I asked Ludwig to teach me how to be a capitalist. And I said while this was possible, said the capitalist, I didn't really want to return to the world of banking because it would be too painful. Just thinking about it made me feel ashamed. I understood his point completely, said the painter. It was also true that while I could train Ludwig to be a painter, I had no wish to return to the world I had fled from either. But then an idea occurred to me, said the capitalist. Just because I couldn't work as a banker didn't mean I had to completely abandon the world of finance. For instance I knew I was still capable of showing someone how to start and run a successful small business. And I realized that even though I had no wish to be associated with the art world any longer, said the painter, I still knew a thing or two about pigments and mixing paint. Then we shook hands and agreed to teach each other the skills we used in our former lives, said the capitalist. And that's how P & C Custom Paints LLC was born, said the painter. The very next day I had movers pack up my office at the bank and transport my things into this building, said the capitalist. And then for the following month we spent our days giving each other lessons, said the painter. Once I felt that I knew enough about mixing paint I drew up a list of materials I needed to get started, said the capitalist. And then I wrote up a business plan to finance it all, said the painter. A month later we had all the equipment we needed and our company was operational, said the capitalist. That's how we found a cure for our illiteracy, said the painter.

That's quite a remarkable story, said Jones. Isn't it? said the capitalist. The advice I have for you involves understanding similar things about yourself, said the painter. Well what you said makes a lot of sense, said Jones. Recently I've had trouble selling my novel, so maybe I'm not cut out to be a fiction writer after all. But some of the articles I've written for the magazine where I work have gotten a lot of attention. My agent thinks I'd be successful if I put together a proposal for a nonfiction book. But the only problem is that this is sort of impossible if I continue to be unable to read any of the words I write. This damn illiteracy really does put a damper on everything! Have you not listened to a word we've said? asked the painter. Of course I have, said Jones. But if you had, said the painter, you'd understand that for you to write in any function again would be impossible. But why? asked Jones. It'd be too painful, said the capitalist. So what do you propose I do then? asked Jones. Well if I was you I'd start thinking about finding a partner, said the painter. A partner? said Jones. Yes, said the capitalist. A person similarly affected by a sort of illiteracy with a different skill set than your own. You know who would be perfect? said the painter. Who? said the capitalist. That mechanic you bumped into the other day when you were visiting your shrink, said the painter. He's a nice fellow, said the capitalist. Poor soul. One day he woke up unable to fix cars anymore and his inabilities have been driving him mad. What does he have to do with me? asked Jones. Well, you see our little business is growing, said the painter. Right now we're looking for a few more employees. In particular, we want to hire an administrative assistant who can also handle writing marketing copy and a warehouse associate who can drive a van and make deliveries. So our thought was that if you can teach this mechanic how to write persuasively, said the capitalist, maybe he can teach you how to maintain a vehicle. What? said Jones. But that's preposterous. Is it? asked the painter. Surely you can understand why we want to keep the ranks of our company open only to our own kind? Sure, said Jones, but I don't know. Take your time and think it over, said the capitalist. But if you're interested you should stick around, said the painter. The mechanic should be here any moment. But how is that possible? asked Jones. Then both the painter and the capitalist looked at Jones as if he had lost his mind. Well, said the painter, last time Ludwig saw him at his psychiatrist's he mentioned we had an opening. The mechanic seemed interested, so I scheduled an interview with him tonight. We have a large production run starting tomorrow, said the capitalist. Tonight is the only night we have free for the next few weeks, said the painter.

The painter and the capitalist stared at Jones awaiting his decision, but the more he thought about it, the more Jones couldn't bear to meet this mechanic or stay in the warehouse any longer. He wanted to explain himself to these men, who despite the strangeness of their proposition had been kind to him and had taken an interest in his future, but his mind went blank. In the distance he heard the doorbell ring. It must be the mechanic, said the painter. I'll get it, said Jones. Then both men crossed their arms and smiled.

Jones walked out of the warehouse and headed back down the cinder block corridor toward the door and opened it. Outside he saw a man about his age wearing a gas station jacket with a name patch on the left breast that read Smitty. Hi, said Jones. You must be the mechanic? That's right, said the man. Well nice to meet you, said Jones. He extended his hand. I'm the illiterate. The illiterate? said the mechanic, shaking Jones's hand. Yep, said Jones. Please, come in. The gentlemen are expecting you.

The mechanic walked past Jones and headed down the hall. At first Jones started to follow him, but then he thought better of it and bolted out the door. Once he was outside he ran as fast as he could up the street. Half a dozen blocks later he spotted a subway station and darted up to the platform two steps at a time, too nervous to look back to see if the mechanic or the painter or the capitalist had come after him. He had the good luck to catch a train just as it was arriving at the station. After the doors closed Jones looked back to the street and saw that it was just as empty as it had been when he sprinted through it moments before. He wasn't sure what to do, so he decided he should just go home.

CHAPTER 10: THE PHONE CALLS

Could any of this really be happening? Jones wondered. *How has my life spun so far out of control?* After living with his illiteracy for just a week Jones felt more tired than he had ever been in his entire life. More than anything he needed some rest.

Jones had a quick glass of whiskey when he got home from the painter's. Then he went to sleep and stayed in bed the next day too. Jones decided it was in his best interest to hibernate for a little while. Though he took a few breaks to smoke joints and eat the occasional bowl of cereal, he popped sleeping pill after sleeping pill, and only after living this way for over a week did Jones wake up refreshed one fine morning prepared to deal with his fate.

After showering, Jones made a pot of coffee and turned on the news. It was sunny outside and his apartment felt stuffy, so he opened the window. He noticed the air smelled of spring. *My spring as well,* Jones thought. The season of rebirth had arrived and he felt ready. Jones grabbed his jacket and walked toward his door. He noticed a pile of notes had accumulated in front of it. He picked one up but he still couldn't make out any of the words. Then he looked back down to the pile of notes. There seemed to be so many. *Have people been trying to visit me?* Jones wondered. When he thought about it, vague recollections of people pounding on the door came back to him, but he guessed he must have just ignored them all. For a moment he considered comparing some of the notes to the translation chart he'd made, but then he felt another spring breeze come through the window and thought better of it. The time had come for him to face the day and to face himself and finally get to the bottom of this illiteracy. Jones kicked the notes aside and headed out the door.

Outside the day was even nicer than he imagined it would be. The shops along 5th Avenue were just opening and everyone he passed on the sidewalk seemed to be in a good mood. Jones didn't have anywhere he had to be, but after spending so many days indoors he felt like taking a long walk, so he started heading toward the Brooklyn Bridge. Maybe he would cross over it into the city and then head north into Chinatown to a good Vietnamese place he knew and grab a bowl of pho for lunch. The simplicity of his plan relaxed Jones and gave him something to look forward to, so he happily set off toward the bridge.

Then Jones felt something vibrate in his pocket and pulled out his cell phone. He hadn't answered it in days and was shocked to find that he had over twenty messages. I've never been so popular before, Jones said with a chuckle. He pushed the button for them to play.

*

The first was from Caroline. Jones, please call me back right away, she said. I'm just so worried about you. How'd the doctor's go? Are you OK? I stopped by your apartment, but I guess you weren't there? Anyway, call me. I love you.

Dear Caroline, Jones thought. It had been cruel of him to avoid her as he had. After all, she deserved to be kept in the loop of what was happening to him. Jones made a mental note to call her as soon as he finished listening to the rest of his messages.

*

The next was from his editor. As soon as Jones heard his voice he trembled. Jones, said the editor, I'm calling to say sorry about the other day. It's been tense times around here and I've always been able to depend on you to perform, so I guess everything that's been happening with your health caught me by surprise. My point is I was out of line. You always give it your all, so I can understand that maybe you're just exhausted. Take all the time you need to recover, but please give me a quick call to touch base. I need to know if your absence will be short-term or long-term because I need to make a plan.

Finally people are behaving reasonably again, Jones thought. *Finally they aren't blaming me for my condition.* He made a note to call his editor as well and pushed the button for the next message.

*

It was from his agent. Hey there, said his agent. Call me. I have good news. Since you haven't been around I took the liberty of repackaging your material. I wrote a proposal for a nonfiction book. It'd be an anthology of five of your most popular features from the magazine along with five new essays. I know you're probably freaking out, but listen; I packaged them with your novel as a two-book deal. The only variable left to determine is which book would be best to publish first. But I've made the rounds and there is definitely some interest. I need to know when you're around so I can schedule some meetings.

Jones was shocked. His agent might be able to sell his novel? *Is it possible that so much happened while I was asleep?* he wondered. There was still the problem of his illiteracy to deal with, but maybe he could use his condition to his advantage and claim that writing the book had caused him to lose his ability to read? And then there were the other essays to write. But maybe he could dictate them. *How strange this life is,* Jones thought. *Just when you're down and out, everything has a way of coming together.*

*

He played the next message. It was from a woman, but at first he didn't recognize the voice. Hey, she said. I've been thinking about you since yesterday. I mean, wow. That was, umm, intense. Then she exhaled into the phone. Instantly Jones knew it was Veronica. I want to see you tonight, she continued. I'll be at the bar after 5 again. Bring more speed.

Just listening to Veronica's voice gave Jones an erection as he walked. He was tempted to stop listening to his messages and call her back at once. But then he thought about the drugs. He reached inside his jacket, but he couldn't find the pill bottle anywhere. *Shit,* Jones thought. He remembered he'd given the pills to the painter but had forgotten to ask for them back. *Well, maybe I can get another prescription from the psychiatrist?* Jones thought. He made a note to call the doctor later. Even if he had to put things off with Veronica for a day or two, he assumed he could always call the bar and explain.

*

The next message was from his assistant. She spoke fast and seemed worried. Hey, it's me, she said. I don't mean to bother you, but I haven't heard from you in almost two weeks. Is everything OK? How'd the ophthalmologist's go? Call me if you can. I'm not really sure what I should be doing with you not around. Also, your editor keeps bugging me. He keeps asking if I've heard from you. I'll tell him anything you want, but I thought it would be best to check in with you so we're on the same page. Feel better.

Jones was surprised at how loyal his assistant seemed to be despite what had occurred. It seemed strange that his editor was asking about him, but then again he supposed that was natural enough. After all, what else did his editor and assistant have to talk about?

Jones made a note to check in with his assistant when he had a chance. Perhaps he'd reward her loyalty with some of his smaller writing assignments. *Yes,* he thought, *that's exactly what I'll do.* Jones could see the look on her face. It made him happy.

*

He played the next message, but had no idea who the speaker was. The tone was formal. At first Jones was confused. Mr. Jones, a man said. I wish I'd had more time to speak with you the other night, but it's my hope that we might get together and talk some time soon. It's funny how things happen. It's funny how one morning can change everything and then one conversation can change everything else. Well it's my hope that the conversation we have can be that sort of conversation. Then the man left a number, but Jones still had no idea who it was. By the way, the man continued, this is Smitty. I used to be a mechanic, but I don't do that anymore. We met briefly at the painter's the other night.

Jones was astounded. *The mechanic? Has he been persuaded by the painter and the capitalist to take part in their strange plan?* At first Jones was angry that the mechanic had contacted him, but then he took pity on the man. Though he had only seen him for a few seconds, he had seemed kind. Most likely he hadn't had the advantages Jones had had in life. For all he knew the mechanic might be uneducated. *And what an awful predicament for an uneducated man to be in,* Jones thought. Despite what had occurred, at least Jones knew he had a sound mind. And then there was the question of friends. *Did the mechanic have any?* The messages Jones had listened to so far proved that he still did. They proved that the people closest to him had stood by him even though others thought he'd lost his mind. *And where would I be without my friends?* Jones thought. *Surely I wouldn't be out walking on a beautiful spring morning confident in my abilities to overcome this unfortunate condition?* Jones felt bad for the mechanic.

Maybe the man has a wife and kids? This thought made him feel worse. Jones resolved to call the mechanic back and offer to meet with him. It was the least he could do. Even though he had no interest in working for the painter and the capitalist, he might be able to provide guidance to the confused mechanic. It seemed like the right thing to do.

*

Jones played the next message. It was Caroline again, but now she sounded angry. *I wonder how long she's been trying to get ahold of me?* Jones thought. Hi, she said. So I'm not really sure what to say here. I care about you, but you don't get back to me? This makes me worry so I go to your place, but you don't answer the door. So I call again and leave another message and then I go back to your place and slip another note under the door, only this time I'm pretty sure you're there. Didn't you hear me knocking? I could smell pot smoke and it sounded like you were eating cereal! *Could this be true?* Jones wondered. He tried to remember, but the days he spent sleeping were all a blur. What the hell is wrong with you? Caroline continued. Then she started to cry. If you're around tonight stop by Ruby's. I'll be out with my real friends celebrating. You remember that screenplay I started? Well there's already been some interest in it. I actually signed with your agent yesterday. She thinks it's going to be a big blockbuster.

After the message ended Jones wasn't sure how to react. Had his absence really been responsible for destroying his relationship with Caroline? It had only been a week or two, but he guessed this was possible. Had she really been standing outside his door and heard him eating cereal? It sounded almost too strange for Caroline to have made it up, so Jones assumed it was true. But maybe it was for the best? After all, she'd gone to his agent with her lousy screenplay. *Unbelievable!* Jones thought, as he pressed the button for the next message.

*

It was his editor again, but this time he was yelling. What the fuck? said the editor. I try to be nice, but you still can't call me? I try to be empathetic, but without you at least offering the smallest explanation, how the fuck do you expect me to understand? I am trying to run a business here, you know? But maybe this is more of your superior artistic bullshit. Well, I tell you what, if it is, fine. You can be as artistic as you want for all I care because as far as I'm concerned you're through here. I tell you though, what surprises me the most is your nerve. I can't believe you had the audacity to let your assistant write your column for you today and turn it in under your byline. What, you didn't think I'd notice? Well I did notice. It's actually not bad. Maybe I'll give her your job. She's certainly more pleasant to look at than your sorry ass. Especially when she wears that sexy leather skirt. Then the editor hung up.

Shit, said Jones. He had just reached the promenade in Brooklyn Heights. It was one of his favorite spots, so he stopped for a moment and thought about sitting down on a bench for a minute to collect himself, but it was hopeless. Standing there he felt too consumed by his thoughts to enjoy the view, so he continued north toward the Brooklyn Bridge. *Have I really lost my job?* Jones thought. *And what is this about my assistant turning in her work as my own? Surely all it would take is a few phone calls to sort everything out?* The thing to do would be to call his editor and apologize for his absence right away, but Jones still had at least a dozen messages to listen to, and what if the editor or his assistant had called again?

*

Hey there, the next message started. It sounded like Veronica. What happened to you last night? she continued. Then she let out a slight moan. If I don't see you at the bar tonight I'm going to have to hunt you down. Then Veronica hung up the phone. Jones looked out across the East River at the skyscrapers of Lower Manhattan and was tempted to throw his phone into the water and run to a bar at once. But instead he played the next message.

*

Mr. Jones, said a voice on the next message. Jones didn't recognize it right away. I'm extremely disappointed to hear that you haven't gotten back to the mechanic yet. Then Jones realized that it must be the painter. He's depending on you, the painter continued. We're depending on you too. The least you could do is call me back. We need to know what your decision is. How do you think it looked when you ran away from the mechanic the other night? Then the painter paused. Please let me know what your intentions are as soon as possible. Obviously if you won't accept our offer we'll need to start looking for someone else. If I don't hear from you, I'll be forced to talk to the psychiatrist about our recent interaction. Do I make myself clear? Then the painter hung up.

Is he trying to threaten me? Jones wondered. *And what's this about speaking to the psychiatrist?* Jones was livid. If he had a problem with the psychiatrist then he might have a problem getting more Dexedrine, which meant that he might have a problem seeing Veronica again. Fuck! said Jones. Then he continued on.

*

The next message was from his agent again. So I jumped the gun on that last message I left you, she said. It turns out that editors are only interested in publishing a book of your essays. Everyone says your novel is too complicated, and frankly I don't blame them. I just took another look at it myself and I see their point. It's good, Jones, but hardly marketable. Maybe you should take some pointers from Caroline. Have you seen her screenplay? It's totally genius. If the offers keep coming in I'll have it sold by the weekend. Can you call me? Please?

Too complicated? Take some pointers from Caroline? Jones had a better idea. *Maybe it's time for me to find a new agent.*

*

The next message was from his super. I don't know what the hell your problem is, said the super. For over a week now I've been trying to talk to you about that night when you needed me to let you into the building. It wasn't that big of a deal. I just wanted to show you where I hide a spare set of keys outside. But you don't answer the door when I stop by? You don't answer my notes or my calls? That one time you even slammed the door in my face. Who do you think I am? You think I'm just some little punk? Well think whatever you want. I don't give a shit. I just wanted to give you the heads up that I got my eye on you and one more slipup, say something like the smell of pot in the hallway, and I'm going to do everything I can to get you evicted.

Great, Jones thought. Not only had he lost his job, but now he was destined to be homeless too. *Just great,* Jones thought as he played the next message.

*

He heard an automated voice. This is to verify that you have recently accepted an increase on you credit line. Your new limit is $10,000. If you have not authorized this transaction please contact the fraud-prevention department immediately. Then the voice started to give a number, but Jones cut off the message before it finished.

What the hell? he thought. *Now on top of everything else someone is ripping me off?* Then Jones remembered the old drunk at the bar where Veronica worked. He wished he hadn't given him his credit card. But he could still fix this. He just needed to call and report his card stolen. *Yet another call I need to make,* Jones thought. He felt overwhelmed. He needed to make a list of the people he needed to call, but he was just starting to cross the

Brooklyn Bridge, so he decided to stop at a coffee shop once he got to the other side and figure out everything then. *It's just that all of this is hitting me at once,* he thought. *I need to calm down and keep a cool head.* Jones took a deep breath and looked down at the water. It reflected the sun back at him like a mirror. There wasn't a cloud in the sky and he felt warm so he unbuttoned his jacket and played the next message.

*

It was the mechanic again. You know, said the mechanic, the painter and the capitalist spoke so highly of you, so I guess I'm a little surprised you haven't gotten back to me yet. I'm really trying to not be pissed off, but I sort of am because my future's on the line. So is yours. And maybe that's the point. Maybe not returning my calls is some sick little fucking game you're playing just so when we end up working together you keep the upper hand? Well fuck you! yelled the mechanic. You had your chance to get back to me. Now I'm coming for you.

That does not sound good, Jones thought. *Not good at all.* He had no idea what he should do, so Jones just kept walking and played the next message.

*

It was Veronica again. What do you think I am? she said. You think I'm just some fucking whore? You think I just go and fuck any guy in the goddamn broom closet? It's been three days you asshole. You better be here tonight and you better have the stuff!

Then Jones heard Veronica sobbing before she hung up. *Shit,* Jones thought. *What have I gotten myself involved in?*

*

He played the next message and hoped it wouldn't be any worse than Veronica's had been, but of course it was. I'm going to break your face you slippery little fuck, the message started. Jones didn't recognize the voice. First you rape my employee in the broom closest and now you hold out on her and break her little heart. You better watch your back. If I see you around here again, you're dead. Then the line went silent.

Of course, Jones thought. *Now the bartender is calling me too?*

*

He played the next message, but at first he couldn't make out anything. It sounded like someone's phone had dialed his number accidentally. Then a man started talking, but at first Jones couldn't understand what he was saying because he was slurring his words. Hey, hey just let me talk, said the man. Then he heard a deep phlegmy old man cough. *It must be the drunk,* Jones thought. Hey there you illiterate, he said. Thanks again for that credit card. Hope you don't mind that I upped your limit. I needed to. It's been one hell of a bender. But I'm in jail now, the tombs I think, so I was wondering if you would mind bailing me out? It's a long story, but I got caught pumping a rentboy in the park. I lost your card. I think this fucking pedophile snatched it from me when I passed out in the bullpen. Hope you don't mind the call. I got your number from the bar. Man, they seem pretty pissed off at you over there! Then the drunk started laughing and the message ended.

Fuck! Fuck! Fuck! Jones thought, but then he realized he'd accidentally sworn out loud. A woman, he assumed was a teacher, was walking by him with a group of children toward the Brooklyn Bridge. She shook her head at him as she passed, as if to say: You should be ashamed. But Jones had bigger problems to worry about, so it was easy for him to ignore her and head north at the base of the bridge toward Chinatown. He wanted to call his credit card company right away, but he still had messages to listen to. *How many more can there be?* Jones wondered. *Is it possible that they'll make my life any more miserable than it has already become?*

*

He played the next message. It was from the psychiatrist. Mr. Jones, said the psychiatrist, this is Dr. Johnson calling. Please call me back as soon as you get this message. What I have to speak with you about is extremely urgent, and frankly I'm growing concerned. Today was the fifth consecutive appointment you have missed. Perhaps you don't realize how crucial our sessions will be to your recovery? Also, another patient of mine, Heinrich the painter, has informed me of some questionable behavior on your part. Apparently he reached out and offered you his counsel and even a job, I hear, only to have you laugh at him. He even tells me that you went so far as to spit in his face? I find this behavior of yours to be extremely troubling. Just the other day you seemed so willing to do whatever was necessary to cure your condition, but now you seem to be employing tendencies that seem to be marginally psychopathic. Please call me back at once. If I don't hear from you in 24 hours I will be forced to contact the authorities.

But what authorities was he talking about? Jones wondered. *What had the painter told the psychiatrist? How have I gotten so tangled up in such a strange web of misunderstanding?* Jones realized that fixing things seemed to be growing increasingly difficult. What could he do? Call the psychiatrist? He didn't know. What if the psychiatrist had already spoken with these authorities? Then calling him could lead to his arrest. And on top of this he still had more messages. *Well at least I'm almost at the restaurant,* Jones thought as he approached Canal Street, though now after all the messages lunch was the last thing on his mind.

*

Listen you little prick, you have some explaining to do, the next message started. Jones was shocked. It sounded like the neurologist. First of all I'm candid with you, the doctor continued. Then I go out of my way to refer you to my own psychiatrist. And how do you repay me? You embarrass me. That's how, you little shit. I just got off the phone with Dr. Johnson and he tells me you haven't shown up to any of your appointments. And on top of that you've been toying with his other patients? Well, I'm just calling to warn you that there will be consequences if this behavior persists. And by the way, I took another look at your scans. I think you might have something seriously wrong with you. Good luck with that you fuck! It might be brain cancer for all I know! Then Jones heard the phone smash down onto the receiver so hard it hurt his ear.

Consequences? Jones thought. *But what did he mean by that? And now there might be something wrong with my head? Was he serious? Are my doctors really harassing me just because I slept through a few appointments?* Jones was confused. He walked right past the restaurant he had intended to stop at and headed farther north toward the Lower East Side where he liked to hang out and drink.

*

Hello, the next message started. It was a woman's voice. She sounded old. This is Mrs. Watson calling. I run a pharmacy in Brooklyn that you visited a few days ago. Perhaps you remember stopping by my store to fill a prescription for Dexedrine? I remember you. I remember that you were rude. Jones was confused. *Why is the pharmacist calling me?* Jones wondered. *This is ridiculous.* Well, the woman continued, I just couldn't resist calling you. After you left my store, I couldn't get over how ungrateful you'd acted. Your attitude bothered me so much I mentioned you to my family at dinner that night. And I tell you, it's funny how things work out sometimes. After I mentioned you, my daughter Judy told me about a young man fitting your description who spent a few hours hanging out at the coffee shop where she works.

She told me she saw you propositioning her customers with pills. So I just wanted to call you young man and tell you that I have turned your name into the police. Then the old woman laughed and hung up the phone.

Was it possible? Jones wondered. He couldn't believe that the pharmacist and the barista were mother and daughter. It struck him as preposterous. But then again after so many strange messages Jones wasn't so sure anymore what was preposterous and what was not.

*

To his relief Jones heard the automated voice on his phone tell him that he had no more new messages. He had just started crossing Delancey Street. Jones didn't know what to do or think. He was shocked that in a few hours such a lovely day had become so awful. It was almost as if it wasn't happening, like everything he had heard was really just part of some inside joke. *But how can this be?* Jones wondered. He was too nervous and afraid to dismiss the threats he'd heard in the messages. If the police and the medical authorities were after him, he'd have to be careful and watch his step. *But what to do? Where to go?* Jones thought. *Is it even worthwhile to try to fix my reputation? Maybe I'd be better off just running away somewhere to start a new life?* Jones was uncertain. *Maybe I just need some time to think?*

The only thing Jones knew for sure was that he needed a drink.

CHAPTER 11: AT THE BAR

Jones walked into the first bar he saw and drank for hours. The place was a cruddy dive perfectly suited to his temperament. Its interior was painted black and covered with graffiti. Heavy metal blared from the stereo. There were never more than a dozen or so other patrons there and no one bothered him. His only inclination that time was passing was the changing crowd that gradually shifted from the old neighborhood drunks to the younger happy hour folks.

Minutes after Jones sat down at the bar he felt his phone vibrate again. Then he got another call a few minutes after that, and another call every ten minutes or so. With every new phone call he grew more afraid and noticed his hands start to shake. He was tempted to pull out his phone and see who had called, but was uncertain if it was a good idea to fill his head with even more troubling thoughts. In the end he decided to turn his phone off and continue to drink. He thought about throwing his phone away, but he was still sober enough to resist illogical endeavors. Even still, he was bewildered by what had happened. Nothing about it made sense. There was nothing Jones wanted more than a clear resolution, but the longer he sat in the bar drinking, the more confused his thoughts grew, and the self-pity that eventually emerged came easily. *Have I lost my ability to tell the difference between my enemies and my friends too?* Jones wondered. *Is this just another element of my illiteracy?* Jones felt embarrassed by this lapse in his judgment. As a writer he'd always thought of himself as a good judge of character. This failure to see the true intentions of the doctors and all the others made him feel that it was he who had changed and the responsibility for this failure was his own. Sitting there at the bar Jones felt so low. More than anything he felt ashamed.

*

After wasting away in the bar for a few hours Jones decided the time had come for him to be on his way. He wasn't sure if he could go home or not because he was afraid the police might be waiting for him, so he decided to order one final drink and think things over. He signaled the bartender to refill his glass and watched as the man took the bottle from the bar and refilled his Jameson and then also refilled another glass to the left of his own. Jones looked up and found that the owner of this glass was a hideous looking woman who happened to be sitting next to him. He watched her pick up her drink and noticed her fat fingers. On some of her nails there was fingernail polish, but it was mismatched and chipped. Then she raised the glass to her lips and downed the whiskey in one gulp. *How did I end up sitting next to such a hag?* Jones wondered. *I can't believe I didn't notice her until just now!* Just the thought of spending another minute sitting next to this woman disgusted him, so Jones looked around the bar for another seat. But then something caught his eye.

The hag seemed to be wearing sunglasses similar to the ones Veronica had been wearing. Just the sight of them made Jones tremble with fear. *Is it possible this woman is some sort of spy who has been sent after me?* Jones wondered. *Or what if she's been sent to do me harm?* Jones didn't know what to do. He was tempted to run out of the bar, but then it occurred to him that perhaps that was the reaction they had anticipated he'd have, and maybe his doctors and the others were waiting for him outside. *No,* Jones thought. *I won't run. If I really want to get out of this situation I need to confront my enemies head-on.* Jones downed his drink and ordered another. Then he turned toward the hideous lady.

So I see you're wearing sunglasses even though it's already dark outside and even darker in this bar, said Jones. Excuse me? said the woman. *Perfect,* Jones thought, *I've caught her by surprise.* I said I couldn't help but notice you're wearing sunglasses indoors. That's right, said the woman. Well I was in this student bar the other day in Brooklyn and noticed the same thing. What's that? said the woman. People wearing sunglasses indoors, said Jones. It was the weirdest thing. It was earlier than it is now, 4 or 5 o'clock I'd say. But I walked into this bar to meet a friend and found every other patron wearing sunglasses. I didn't want to stick out so I put on my own pair. OK? said the woman. And seeing as you're wearing sunglasses indoors now, I figured you'd be just the person to ask if it's some sort of fad or something? What are you talking about? said the woman. Her voice sounded confused and a little drunk. Jones was elated. He had her exactly where he wanted. I said I was wondering why you're wearing sunglasses inside, Jones continued. Maybe it's some sort of fad popular with the college kids? I wouldn't know, said the woman. Do I look like I'm in college? I guess not, said Jones, but maybe you could just tell me why you're wearing sunglasses inside then? You're really a piece of work, you know? said the woman. Excuse me? said Jones. Einstein, she continued, I'm wearing sunglasses because I'm blind. You're blind? said Jones. He was shocked. He hadn't expected this at all. Yeah, said the woman. I am. Now that you've insulted me, perhaps you'd care to buy me a drink? Of course, said Jones. Then he ordered another round.

Jones wasn't sure what to say to the woman, so he remained silent for a few minutes and just sipped his whiskey. His behavior toward her surprised him. She was, after all, a perfect stranger who had never done a thing to him and there he was insulting her just because he was paranoid after receiving those nasty messages earlier. Now he'd have to come up with something to say to this unattractive stranger in order to explain himself and he didn't know where to start.

Jones turned to the blind woman. Listen, he said, I'm really sorry about all this. Don't worry about it, said the blind woman. It happens all the time. Really? said Jones. Well maybe not quite like this, said the blind woman. People never know how to react to me, but really, it's OK. I'm Delores. Nice to meet you, Jones said. I'm Jones.

The blind woman extended her hand and they shook. Jones couldn't help but notice her hand wasn't as flabby as he thought it would be. Instead it felt soft, and even sensual in a way. I take it you're uncomfortable with my blindness? said the blind woman. Excuse me? said Jones. Or maybe you just didn't expect to encounter a woman with my condition out on the prowl? *Out on the prowl?* Jones thought. *What the hell is she talking about?* Speak up, son, the blind woman continued. One minute you're interrogating me for wearing dark glasses and the next you're silent. What happened? Cat got your tongue? Listen, said Jones. I'm sorry for being so rude. It's hard to explain, but about two weeks ago I woke up illiterate and since then nothing's turned out how I thought it would. Recently I found out that some people I thought were my friends seemed to have turned against me so I've become increasingly paranoid. What? said the blind woman. I know it sounds absurd, said Jones, but the thing is, I guess I suspected you were part of the conspiracy. Wow, said the blind woman, illiterate, huh? How exactly did that happen? I have no idea, said Jones. One morning I woke up unable to read letters and numbers. I've gone to half a dozen doctors but no one knows what's wrong with me. That's bizarre, said the blind woman. It is, said Jones. In a way I almost wish I were completely blind instead. Do you really? said the blind woman. Sure, said Jones. At least then my condition would be easier to explain. That's true, said the blind woman. And blindness does have certain advantages. Yes, I suppose it does, said Jones. Particularly when it comes to lovemaking, the blind woman continued. Hmm, said Jones. Then he turned away from the woman and ordered them another round.

The blind woman's last comment caught Jones off guard and he wasn't sure how to respond. His intention in talking to her was to be polite and to account for the rude way he had treated the woman moments before, yet their conversation seemed to be going toward a place he hadn't anticipated and this interested him.

Jones turned back toward the blind woman and gave her the fresh drink. How exactly does that work? he said. How exactly does what work? said the blind woman. Blind lovemaking, said Jones. Oh, said the blind woman. It's spectacular. Your lack of vision frees up your imagination. Really? said Jones. It doesn't matter who you're actually with because blindness allows you to be with anyone. I suppose that makes sense, said Jones. Here, said the blind woman. She placed her hand on Jones's knee. I want to show you something. Just close your eyes. Close my eyes? said Jones. He was apprehensive about where this was going, but Jones was also feeling a little drunk and a little horny, so he figured what the hell.

All right, they're closed, said Jones. He felt the blind woman slowly move her hands from his leg up the contours of his chest to his face. Her touch was gentle, and Jones began to feel an erection coming on. Dear, you're a cute one, said the blind woman. Then she ran her fingers away from his face back down to his leg. With you not much imagination is required. What do you mean by that? asked Jones. What exactly are you trying to show me? Well it's like this, said the blind woman. Jones felt her hand slip into his crotch. You see I'm no looker, but since I'm blind my appearance doesn't really matter because reality is completely up to me. In a way that's why I suppose this illiteracy is so difficult, said Jones. Because being illiterate is being caught between two worlds. Exactly, said the blind woman. That's why right now I want you to forget your troubles and relax. If you can, pretend you're blind and imagine I'm whoever you want me to be. With those words Jones felt her grip on his crotch tighten. And with her touch he felt his erection grow. Just imagine that I am your secret sexual fantasy, she continued. Imagine that I'm the one you've always wanted but have never conquered. Jones felt the blind woman pull down his zipper. And then: the soft touch of her skin. No longer was she some fat blind hag he was only talking to because he had accidentally insulted her. The reality of where he was faded away and suddenly he felt suspended in space. He closed his eyes tighter and felt her breath on his neck and didn't think about anything. And then: It felt glorious; his only regret was that it hadn't lasted longer.

After it was over Jones didn't know what to do so he sipped his drink. He looked over to the blind woman. She pulled her hand out of his crotch and sipped her own drink. So, what do you think? she said. Remarkable, said Jones. Well if you're game, why don't we get out of here and go somewhere where we can really screw? I'm game, said Jones. He signaled the bartender for his check. Well hold on a second sailor, said the blind woman. Yes? said Jones. Don't you think you ought to stop by the restroom first and clean yourself up? Jones looked down to his lap and blushed. I suppose that would be a good idea, he said. I'll be right back.

Jones zipped up his jeans and headed to the back of the bar to find the bathroom. Walking made him realize that he was a little drunker than he'd thought, but it was nothing a little water in his face couldn't fix. He opened the bathroom door and walked into the men's room. After he cleaned himself off, he urinated. He looked into the mirror. *Well this is certainly a strange turn of events,* Jones thought. Hours before he had felt ready to start a new life for himself and was determined to get to the bottom of his illiteracy, but now here he was about to go home with some fat blind woman who had just given him a hand job in a bar. Well, fuck it, said Jones. Then he splashed some water onto his face, slicked back his hair, and walked out the door.

CHAPTER 12: AN ENCOUNTER WITH THE CONSPIRATORS

Jones walked away from the bathroom ready for whatever lay ahead of him that night. He took a deep breath and headed back down the corridor toward the bar. He knew that he needed to stop thinking about his old life because it didn't matter anymore. He knew that he needed to embrace the present and see where it led and not care about the limitations imposed by his condition.

Jones thought about these things and continued to walk, but he didn't seem to be getting any closer to the bar. The hallway was much longer than he remembered and Jones wondered if it was possible that he had exited out of the wrong door in the bathroom and ended up somewhere else. Instinctually he turned around and headed back toward it. The corridor was dark and he couldn't see where he was going. He looked down to his watch, but he couldn't make out its hands. He had no idea how long he had been wandering around in the dark. Jones worried that the blind woman would leave before he returned and started walking faster. *Or even worse,* he thought, *what if she finds someone else?*

At the end of the hallway Jones encountered a staircase. This surprised him because he didn't remember seeing it before. *Could I have walked past the bathroom door in the darkness?* Jones wondered. He backtracked a few paces, feeling the walls for the door, but he didn't find anything. *So strange,* Jones thought. *After all that has occurred, now I'm lost in the back hallways of a bar?* Jones walked back to the stairs. He seemed to be standing at the top of it, so he started walking down the steps. *Maybe this is just an unmarked exit?* he thought. Jones tried his best to remain optimistic as he descended the stairs, but with each step he grew more afraid.

At the bottom of the stairway there was a door. Above it hung an exit sign. *Perfect,* Jones thought. He opened it. He walked into a room and heard the door close behind him. Shit! said Jones. He tried to push the door back open, but it seemed to be locked. He looked around the room. There were stacks of beer cases and a few kegs in the corner. Up above somewhere Jones heard a car go by. He realized that he was probably in the storage cellar under the sidewalk. *There must be a stairway or ladder to the street,* Jones thought. But he didn't see anything. Then in the distance somewhere he heard a person laugh. Jones started walking toward the voice. At the other end of the storage cellar he found another door. It was unlocked, so Jones opened it and found another stairway. He heard more laughing and some people talking. The sound seemed to be coming from the top of the stairs, so he ascended them. Once he reached the top, Jones looked around and realized that he was in the back room of the bar. He saw discarded beer cases and piles of trash. Jones noticed a faint light shining through a curtain hanging on the far side of the room. It seemed to be concealing another area. Jones walked closer. With each step he took the voices grew clearer.

What *don't* you understand about this? a man said. You're ruining my life. If you don't get back to me, you better believe I'm going to ruin yours! Jones recognized the voice, but he wasn't sure where it was from. Then he heard the same voice chuckle. What do you think? the man continued. That was OK, I guess, said another man. Just OK? said the first. Well, I mean it was frightening, but your threat was a little cliché, said the second. I agree, said a third voice. Why not try something like this? Jones recognized the other two voices too. He edged forward.

Beyond the curtain Jones found a dark room. In the middle of it was a circular table full of beer bottles, around which sat about ten people. The room was illuminated only by a single light bulb that hung above the table. At first Jones had a hard time seeing the people at the table and had no idea who was there. Watch and learn my friends, the third voice continued. Jones squinted his eyes and looked over to the speaker. He recognized him. It was the psychiatrist. Jones was shocked. He froze and watched his doctor talk into a cell phone. Mr. Jones, said the psychiatrist, though now his voice assumed a heavy Brooklyn accent. This is Lieutenant Biggs calling from the 88th Precinct. Your failure to call us back is only making the case against you worse, and frankly it's starting to piss me off. You better hope one of our guys doesn't pick you up! Then the psychiatrist put down the phone. Not bad Johnson, said another man. Not bad at all. Thanks Pace, said the psychiatrist. *Pace?* Jones thought. *Dr. Pace is my neurologist. Is it really him?* Jones wondered. He thought it was but he couldn't tell for sure, so he got down on his hands and knees and crawled under the curtain. He stayed low in the shadows and was careful not to make a sound as he entered that room. Closer now, Jones looked back at the table and found that it was in fact the neurologist. He was seated to the left of the psychiatrist. And then he saw the painter and the mechanic sitting next to the psychiatrist on the right. *Can it be possible?* Jones thought. He couldn't believe that so many of his adversaries had gathered there. Does anyone else have any good ideas? said the neurologist. I'm drained. I have one, said a woman, sitting to the neurologist's left. Jones pivoted in the shadows to see who was speaking and saw that it was Veronica. *But how does she know my doctors?* Jones wondered. He watched as she pulled out her cell phone and dialed. It's me again you dirty motherfucker, said Veronica. If you don't call me back, I'm calling the cops. Oh, and by the way, I noticed something down there this morning. I swear, if you gave me anything I'll kill you! she screamed. Someone Jones couldn't see broke out into a little chuckle. Then again it might have been a few people laughing at once. Jones wasn't sure. How was that? asked Veronica. OK, said the neurologist, but we need to be more creative. I could threaten to fire him again, said another voice. It sounded like his editor. *But that's impossible,* thought Jones. Then he crawled a little closer to the table and found that he was correct. The editor was sitting to the left of Veronica and next to him Jones spotted his assistant. *So they've all conspired against me?* Jones thought. I don't know how effective that would be, said the psychiatrist. We could go wreck his place? asked another voice. Jones moved a bit farther along the floor and turned to the new speaker. It was a teenager flanked by three other boys. Jones recognized them instantly. They were the kids from the wine store who had stolen his keys. *But how could they be involved in this?* he wondered. *They don't know who I am. They certainly don't know about my condition.* Don't you boys listen? said the neurologist. We've already had the super change his locks, so the fact that you possess his keys is completely useless. Furthermore we've positioned Caroline and the bartender in the coffee shop across the street from his building. We haven't heard anything from them yet, have we? No, said the assistant. Not a peep. Well keep checking in with them, said the neurologist. That's really the best thing we have going for us. Then everyone seated around the table laughed.

Suddenly it all became clear to him. Jones understood what his conspirators had planned and grew enraged. He saw it happening before his eyes. His apartment building was in the distance and he could feel how tired he would be as he approached it. When he reached the door, he felt his frustration when his key wouldn't turn in the lock and his powerlessness when he pulled out his phone, unsure who to call. He couldn't call his super. But maybe he could call Caroline. Had he ever gotten around to giving her a key to his place? Then he would see her walking toward him from the coffee shop across the street. She'd be crying. Darling, she would say. But then again maybe she wouldn't say anything. Maybe they would just embrace. Jones was certain of that. Before he could apologize for avoiding her, she'd pull out his spare set of keys, as if she had just known he was locked out. Then he would take the keys from her and walk toward the door. Out of the corner of his eye he would see the bartender running toward him. Maybe he would be shouting. Then again maybe he would be silent. Maybe Caroline would see him and act afraid. But maybe her indifference would be obvious. Jones would see the man running toward him and try the key again and again, but it wouldn't work.

Maybe it would break off in the lock, but that might be pushing it. In the end Jones's impending altercation with the bartender wouldn't matter because just as he was tackled to the sidewalk a police car would pull up. Then Jones would be arrested because the pharmacist's daughter had seen him offering drugs to younger girls he didn't know.

As Jones thought about these things the laughter at the table grew louder. It was almost as if his adversaries could read his mind. They laughed so loud it became impossible for him to think. *There's only one thing for me to do,* Jones thought. He stood up and faced them. How dare you conspire against me? Jones shouted. But the conspirators continued to laugh. What is the meaning of this gathering? asked Jones. But again, his question was ignored. Stop laughing! he continued. If you could only just quiet down for a moment so I can think? But the conspirators kept laughing. Then Jones had an idea. He pulled out his phone. Do you think what you're doing means anything to me? he said. It's been off for hours! And now it will be off forever!

Jones threw his phone as hard as he could into the brick wall behind the table. The conspirators ducked as the phone flew over their heads. It smashed into a million pieces when it hit the wall. Well that was stupid, said the psychiatrist. Why is that? asked Jones. Because you'll just end up buying another phone tomorrow, said the psychiatrist. But how can you be sure about that? asked Jones. Because I know you better than you know yourself, said the psychiatrist. Jones noticed that the others all nodded when he said this. *So he must be the leader,* Jones thought. What do you know about me that I don't know? asked Jones. Before answering Jones's question the psychiatrist paused a moment. Then he stroked his goatee and smiled. I know that the only reason you're here right now is because you have absolutely no idea what you really want, he said. What I really want? said Jones. What's that got to do with anything? I'm only here now because you won't stop tormenting me. And why do you think we've been tormenting you? said the psychiatrist. I have no idea, said Jones. I must say I am astounded by our dear patient's selfishness, said the neurologist. But what does it matter if I'm selfish or not? What does that have to do with this? said Jones. Well, said the psychiatrist, perhaps a better question to ask might be why do you keep changing your mind? I'm not sure I follow, said Jones. One moment you ask us for help, and the next you act like a fool, said the psychiatrist. I couldn't have said it better, said the neurologist. Can't you see your indecision is making it difficult for us to take your condition seriously? said the psychiatrist. After wasting so much of our time, what do you expect us to think? And you think this justifies the threatening messages you left me? said Jones. Isn't it unbelievable, said the painter. He jumped up and pointed at Jones. He still doesn't have a clue! Then he laughed at Jones and the other conspirators joined in.

At first Jones felt confused by the accusations of the conspirators, but the more he thought about them, he couldn't help but agree. While it was true that he had expressed a desire to change his life and move past his illiteracy, maybe it was also true that Jones didn't want to change his life at all. And here he had drawn all these strangers into his struggle and subsequently wasted their time. Jones was shocked by his carelessness, but even still, he didn't think the conspirators' harassment was warranted. Listen, said Jones. You have accused me of being indecisive, and maybe there's some truth in that. But here now I know precisely what I want. I want to leave this strange place and I want all of you to stay away from me and to stop meddling in my affairs. Bravo, finally some decisive action, said the psychiatrist. But don't you understand that the only reason you're here right now is because *you* want to be here right now? You must be out of your mind, said Jones. Hardly, said the psychiatrist. I find it difficult to believe that anyone would want to get lost in a bar and find themselves face-to-face with their adversaries, who they discover are in the midst of conspiring against them, said Jones. It is a rather strange scenario to desire, said the psychiatrist, but you have to agree that your present circumstances do give you an excuse to act any way you wish. Excuse me? asked Jones. Here now, said the psychiatrist, you have an excuse for everything. But why would I need an excuse to be angry with people who have betrayed me? asked Jones. We never betrayed you, said the neurologist. Don't you understand? asked the psychiatrist. I guess I don't, said Jones. You betrayed yourself, said the neurologist. And how did I do this? asked Jones. By dealing with your illiteracy the wrong way, said the psychiatrist. So I shouldn't have informed any of you of my condition or asked for your help? said Jones. Well you might have avoided the entire thing if you had lived a different way, said the neurologist. And how exactly should I have conducted myself? said Jones. He still doesn't know, said the psychiatrist. Then all the conspirators started laughing again. Stop it! yelled Jones. But his pleas only made them laugh harder. I don't have to take this from any of you, said Jones. So don't, said the psychiatrist. If you don't like it here, then get the hell out!

The psychiatrist gestured to his right. Jones saw another door. He was surprised he hadn't noticed it earlier. He looked back to the table. When the conspirators saw the blank expression on Jones's face they laughed the hardest he had heard them laugh all night. Jones couldn't take it anymore. He rushed toward them. He picked up their table and flipped it over. The beer bottles on top of it went flying and some of the conspirators fell to the floor. But the laughter continued. It was deafening. For a moment Jones wanted to kill them all, but instead he ran out of the room.

*

The door led to a small vestibule where Jones found another door. He pushed it open and saw that it led to the street. His first thought was that he needed to go somewhere he could be alone and digest what had just occurred, but then he remembered the blind woman and rushed back to the front of the bar.

Inside the window Jones spotted her sitting on the same stool where he'd encountered her earlier. Looking at her, Jones felt disgusted with himself. Soberer now, he couldn't believe that he had allowed the blind woman to do what she had to him. It was almost as unbelievable as the fact that he had just encountered his conspirators in the back room of a bar. Jones didn't know what to think or believe so he tried to focus on where he was and what he wanted to do. He looked back into the window at the blind woman and saw that she had already started talking to another man. *Well I guess she moves fast,* Jones thought. Just for the hell of it he looked directly into her sunglasses. *She can't see me, so what does it matter if I stare?* Jones thought. Then he waved good-bye, and, to his surprise, he saw her nod toward him. *But that's not possible,* Jones thought. *She must have just happened to nod in my direction.* Jones watched as she lowered her hand from the bar and began caressing the man she was talking to just as she had caressed him an hour or so before. Jones thought about his own hand job and winced. *I need to get out of here,* he thought. Jones took one last look at the blind woman before he walked away. Oddly she seemed to nod to him again, and he wasn't certain, but he could have sworn he saw her smile.

Jones headed down the sidewalk away from the bar. *Somehow I ended up getting lost in the back room of a bar and now I learn that the blind woman who caressed my crotch may not have been blind at all?* Jones thought. *Such a strange place I've ended up tonight. Who would have ever thought my day would end up like this?* Then Jones couldn't help himself. He began to laugh.

Jones knew he'd have time to figure out what had just occurred to him later, but with each step he took he became increasingly uncertain if anything had in fact occurred at all, and as he walked away from the bar he realized that what had or hadn't actually happened didn't matter anymore. Neither did anything else that had occurred since discovering his illiteracy days before. Jones told himself that it all was in the past now, and that he was ready for whatever lay ahead. Then he told himself to shut up and stop thinking.

*

Jones wandered around the city for hours. It was late and he knew he should just go home, but he was afraid the conspirators would be waiting for him there. *Maybe they've notified the police?* Jones thought. He guessed he could just walk around all night, but he knew at some point he'd grow tired. Jones thought about finding a hotel, but hotels were expensive and since he wasn't sure if he was employed any longer, Jones figured he should be careful with money. He started thinking about finding a diner open 24 hours, where he could sit around and drink coffee until daybreak. But what would he do to kill the time? *I obviously can't read the papers,* he thought.

On one corner Jones passed an advertisement for an exotic cruise. He'd never been on one before, but found the idea of a vacation attractive. Even if he didn't take a vacation, maybe he could find a way to spend a few hours sitting on a warm beach. But it was the middle of March and he was in the middle of New York City. Each possibility presented its own problems. Each idea Jones entertained affirmed how lost he felt and how much his life had changed. Just a few weeks before at this very moment he would have been fast asleep in his bed. But now here he was wandering the streets. Jones realized he could confront his conspirators again and try to figure out a way back into his old life, but he wasn't sure he wanted to. Jones knew he needed to go somewhere. He knew he had to do something with his life even if that meant ending it. At the very least Jones knew he had to get off the street.

A block ahead Jones spotted a subway entrance. He decided to walk down the steps into it even though he had no idea where he wanted to go. The station was deserted so he hopped over the turnstile without paying even though he had a MetroCard in his wallet. *Just for the fuck of it,* Jones thought. *Just to fuck with this goddamn city that has fucked with me.* He wasn't sure where he was headed, and the more he thought about it he didn't care. Standing there on the subway platform the only thing Jones was certain of was that he had to take a piss. *I might as well,* he thought. Then Jones opened his fly and started urinating off the platform. He watched his piss splatter off the metal rails and noticed a sign warning about the high voltage of the third rail in the center of the tracks. He wondered if he could hit it with his piss. Then he realized it didn't matter if he could hit it or not because there was no one else around to witness his triumph or his failure.

In the distance he heard a train approaching. He watched the rails below begin to quiver. He still had time to do what he wanted to do. At that moment he understood that there would always be time to do what he wished. So he stood there and continued to piss and felt better than he had in weeks.

As the train got closer Jones stepped back from the edge of the platform and saw that it was an F train headed to Coney Island. *Well maybe I'll go to the beach after all,* Jones thought. When the train stopped he walked onto it and took a seat in the empty subway car. Then the train took off into the tunnels beyond the station and it was only minutes before Jones was fast asleep.

CHAPTER 13: AT THE BEACH

The next morning Jones woke up feeling well rested despite the strange way the past 24 hours had unfolded. He was still sitting on the subway train from the night before, though it didn't seem to be moving any longer. Jones looked around and saw that it was empty except for him. *That's strange,* Jones thought, as he stood up and stretched. He scratched his stubble and tried to figure out where he was. The doors of the train car he was in were all closed so he couldn't walk out onto the platform, but he looked out the window and saw that the sun was out and it looked like it was going to be a beautiful day. *Well I suppose I'll just have to find another way out of here,* Jones thought.

Jones headed to the end of the train car and opened the door into the adjoining one and entered it. At the far end of the next car he spotted a subway employee cleaning the car. *I guess I'm either at the end of the line or the beginning,* Jones thought. *Or maybe the beginning of the end?* He laughed at his observation. He saw the subway employee turn to him. Good morning, said Jones. Then he waved. The subway employee rolled his eyes and looked at him as if he thought he was mad. Jones continued toward the man, but before he was halfway through the car the subway employee pulled out a big set of keys and stuck one into the side panel of the train. Instantly the doors opened. Thank you sir, said Jones. Then he made a bow and pretended to take off an imaginary hat. Toodaloo, Jones continued. He placed the imaginary hat back on his head and headed out the door. He had never been the sort to do ridiculous things, *but fuck it,* Jones thought.

Jones turned away from the train and started down the platform. The air smelled of salt and in the distance he could hear amusement park rides. *I must be in Coney Island,* Jones thought. *Here I am at the beach. Maybe this is where my illiteracy has been driving me all along?* Jones looked around for a trash can. Once he spotted one he reached inside and found a newspaper. He glanced at it and found that nothing about his condition had changed. Jones was disappointed, but not overly so. *Well, I guess this is just how things will be from now on,* he thought. *At least out here my conspirators won't be able to find me.* Then Jones decided to walk to the beach.

*

The season was still too early to attract the crowds of summer, but it was sunny out and the temperature felt unseasonably warm, so Jones wasn't surprised by all the people out and about. He noticed many children walking around too, so he guessed it must be a Saturday or a Sunday. He walked away from the subway station and started for the boardwalk. He liked being where he was. Jones enjoyed being out among strangers who had no knowledge of his illiteracy.

His only plan was to head to the beach, get some sun and take the rest of the day moment by moment, but as he walked through the amusement park it occurred to him that he should probably buy any provisions he might need out on the sand. He wasn't hungry, which struck him as odd considering the absurd amount of alcohol he had consumed the night before, but maybe the awful smell of greasy food that filled the air explained this. He'd always had a sensitive stomach and tried to keep his diet simple. *I should probably buy some water,* Jones thought. And then he wondered if maybe he'd be able to find a little pot. *Wouldn't that be nice?* Jones thought. *Just to lay around today and get high on the beach.* This idea enticed Jones, but he didn't have any idea where to find drugs in the amusement park. He walked slower and made eye contact with the groups of older adolescents he passed, especially those he thought looked slightly criminal, and it was only a matter of time before Jones heard someone ask him: Hey mister, you trying to get high?

Jones stopped walking and found a group of half a dozen tough-looking punk rockers slouching on a boarded-up stand for an amusement park game. As he approached them a lanky boy with a fire engine red Mohawk stepped toward him. *This must be their leader,* Jones thought. He nodded at the youth and reached out to shake his hand, but the leader of the punks stood still. Jones was surprised. *Have drug dealers lost their etiquette too?* he wondered. He looked into the young punk's eyes. They were red and focused on something very far away. *Well,* Jones thought, *that explains it. Clearly he's high as a kite. Hopefully a sign that his product is strong?* Hi, said Jones. I couldn't help but notice your rather generous offer. What are you looking for? said the leader of the punks. It's funny, Jones continued, just moments before I heard you I realized that there is nothing I want to do more right now than go get high on the beach. It's almost as if you read my mind. I got coke, dope, meth, weed, and doses, said the leader. A little weed would be perfect, said Jones. Just a 20 bag then? asked the punk. Sounds good, said Jones. Then he reached for his wallet, but his wallet wasn't there.

Jones always kept his wallet in the front right pocket of his pants, but instead of finding it he saw a slash in his jeans. It went from just below the top of his pocket down to the middle of his thigh and revealed his boxer shorts and his bare leg. It looked like someone had sliced open his pants with a knife. Jones was shocked that he hadn't noticed it before. Even still, he searched his other pockets for his wallet in vain.

Is there a problem, mister? said the leader. I think I've been robbed, said Jones. Really? said the leader, barely concealing a laugh. Yes, Jones continued. It looks like someone has cut my wallet out of my pants. Well let's have a look? said the leader. I can't believe this, said Jones. He showed the punks the hole in his pants. I just noticed this now, but it must have happened last night when I passed out on the train. It's a pity, said the leader. What is? said Jones. That the trains just aren't a safe place for drunks anymore, said another punk. But you got to admire that guy's craftsmanship, said another punk. His craftsmanship? said Jones. Hey mister, said the leader, you mind if we take a closer look?

Jones barely heard the punk's question. He was confused by their sudden interest in his predicament and embarrassed that he had walked around all morning without noticing his pants had been cut. His instinct was to run back to the subway station to look for his wallet and maybe file the appropriate reports with the police, but lacking proper identification and suffering from illiteracy this seemed like a bad idea. All he wanted to do was get high on the beach. *Was that so hard to ask for?* Jones wondered. *But maybe if I cooperate, the punks will give me some weed for free?* He turned back to the leader.

Excuse me? said Jones. I said, you mind if we take a closer look? said the leader. Not at all, said Jones. The leader turned to his gang. Hey Old Chippy, what do you think of this? Jones saw a short punk who looked much older than the rest of the gang step forward. He seemed to have a permanent hunch in his back and it looked like he was losing his hair. He walked forward and nodded at Jones before looking down at the slash in Jones's pants. He knelt down and retrieved a pair of reading glasses from the inside pocket of his leather jacket. He examined the tear closely and slowly moved his fingers along the frayed denim of Jones's pants down to the exposed parts of Jones's boxer shorts and his leg. Jones certainly didn't expect the punks to look at his slashed pants so thoroughly, but Old Chippy behaved extremely professionally throughout his examination, so Jones guessed he couldn't complain. *Clearly this Old Chippy is an expert of some sort,* he thought.

Old Chippy stood back up and turned to the leader. Well, well, said Old Chippy, this is a professional job if I've ever seen one. A professional job? asked Jones. Yes, said Old Chippy. Just look at the tear. Look how clean it is. There's little fraying and the cut is straight. Whoever did this knew exactly what they were doing. And notice that there is no damage to his boxer shorts or his leg. I'd love to examine the wallet as well, but my guess is that unless it was exceptionally bulky, it wouldn't have a scratch on it from the blade. It's actually pretty thin, said Jones. Which plays exactly into what I believe most likely occurred, said Old Chippy. Really? said Jones. Yes, said Old Chippy. I'd say after our thief spotted you snoozing, he tiptoed up to you, located your wallet, and then lightly placed his fingers on the top of your pocket, where the denim is stitched and more difficult to cut. Then he gently pulled up just enough so the fabric was taut and stuck his blade into your pants right below the pocket stitches before sliding it toward him. Slicing your pants in this fashion would leave the long clean cut we have here and allow our thief to grab your wallet and move on to the next train car in ten seconds at most.

Old Chippy turned back to the gang. Can anyone guess what sort of blade was used? What about a big one like this? said one punk. Jones looked over to him and saw that he was holding an open switchblade. Good guess, said Old Chippy, but impossible. Does anyone know why? No one answered. Then Old Chippy took the switchblade from the punk and turned toward Jones. Would you mind if I gave a small demonstration? I suppose that would be all right, said Jones. Excellent, said Old Chippy. Then he turned back to the punks and ran the edge of the blade lightly across his hand. The switchblade is a very fine weapon. From the feel of this one, I'd say that it's certainly sharp enough to make the cut in this man's pants. But its design is better suited for stabbing. Then he turned toward Jones and pulled the fabric of his jeans near the tear taut. You see, if you use a switchblade to try to cut a man's pants open while they are sleeping, you run the risk of accidentally stabbing him in the thigh. The blade's too long. Old Chippy gripped the switchblade downward in his fist and inserted it into Jones's pants. He pulled it toward him and made a slash parallel to the original tear. Also notice that gripping it downward like this can be awkward and take away from the fluidity a job like this demands. But what if you gripped it upward with the blade starting at your thumb? asked one punk. Old Chippy changed his grip on the switchblade and inserted it into Jones's pants again and shredded them some more. Well you could try to do it this way, said Old Chippy, but it's an awkward angle for this sort of grip. Cutting this way often produces wrist cramps.

Old Chippy turned to the gang and handed the switchblade back to its owner. Does anyone else have any other ideas? he asked. What about this knife? said another punk. Jones watched as the young man handed Old Chippy a box cutter. He was amazed. *This gang of drug dealing punks is really serious about their cutting,* he thought. Now we all know that a box cutter can be a useful weapon, said Old Chippy, especially if you find yourself in the sort of situation that requires you to conceal your blade. For approaching a sleeping victim on a train a cutter would be an excellent choice. You can slide it up your sleeve or stick it in your watchband for easy access. If your victim should wake up before you reach him you can easily pass without arousing any suspicion. Yes, the cutter is a useful tool indeed, but certainly not the blade that was used on our friend here. Old Chippy turned back to Jones. You mind? he said. Jones shook his head. Old Chippy took hold of his pants and inserted the cutter next to the two other tears. You see, the problem with the cutter is its length. It's too short to permit the leverage that makes this cut on his pants so smooth. When using a box cutter for this sort of theft, the criminal needs to be extremely careful cutting the denim and constantly make sure that the fabric is taut. Old Chippy pulled the blade toward him to demonstrate. Often an instrument like this will leave the fabric slightly jagged. Also having to constantly adjust your grip on the denim, you risk waking your victim. Then he turned back to the gang. Does anyone have any other ideas?

Jones watched the gang of punks, but no one said anything. Pathetic, said the leader. He turned to Old Chippy and then to Jones. I've tried my best to teach these dumb bastards the tools of our trade, but they don't know a damn thing. It's almost as if they were all illiterate. Well, said Jones, I can certainly understand that. It's complicated, but just the other day the same thing happened to me. Huh? said the leader. What are you talking about? I woke up illiterate about two weeks ago, said Jones, so I find it easy to empathize with you and your disappointment with your gang. Well that's strange, said the leader. What is? said Jones. My illiteracy or my empathy? What do you think? said the leader.

Then the leader continued speaking without giving Jones a chance to answer him. Some days I think I'd be better off without a gang, the leader continued. Some days I wake up and wonder what things would be like today if it was still just me and Old Chippy. Sir, said Old Chippy, I'm sorry to interrupt, but how would you like me to proceed? Just show these idiots how a job like this should be done, said the leader. Then he kicked a discarded beer can lying on the ground.

At the sound of this order Old Chippy's face lit up. *What a character this old punk is*, Jones thought. *This is clearly a man who knows a thing or two about robbing people on the subway with knives.* Old Chippy turned toward Jones.

He smiled at him, so Jones smiled too. He noticed his reflection in Old Chippy's right eye. *Was his eye made of glass?* Jones wondered. Old Chippy pulled an X-Acto knife out of his leather jacket and spun around to face the gang. Gentleman, said Old Chippy, here in my hand I hold the ultimate criminal tool. It's small and not the most intimidating of weapons, but robbing drunks on the train demands not intimidation, but stealth. For it is the agile thief who can jump onto a car with half a dozen passed-out drunks and clean them all out in less than a minute, not the thief who employs brash force. So you see, he continued turning back toward Jones, this is the tool I believe to be responsible for cutting your pants. Then Jones watched Old Chippy slip the knife up his sleeve. Like a box cutter, it's easy to conceal. Then with a flick of his wrist the knife flew into his hand. But like a switchblade, its steel is sharp and strong, said Old Chippy. Then he turned back to Jones. If you'll permit it, one final demonstration? Though Jones was tempted to back away from the gang, he nodded for Old Chippy to go on. Then the old punk grabbed the top of the left front pocket of Jones's jeans. He inserted the tip of the X-Acto knife into the denim and pulled it back toward him, making a cut identical to the original tear on Jones's right pant leg. Craftsmanship, gentleman, said Old Chippy, true craftsmanship can only be achieved with an X-Acto knife. Then Old Chippy bowed and the rest of the gang clapped.

Jones knew he should just run away, but he still wanted to get some weed from the punks. He couldn't believe he had allowed Old Chippy to cut up the other leg of his pants. Hey, said Jones, what the hell? Excuse me? said Old Chippy. Why'd you have to slice open the good leg of my pants? said Jones. Shut up, said the leader. He took a step toward Jones. Then Jones looked over to Old Chippy, who nodded to the leader, as if to hold him off. Old Chippy faced Jones and unzipped his leather jacket. Inside there were at least a hundred X-Acto knives attached to the lining. On the right side Jones noticed a mesh pocket that contained a small brown leather object. *Is that my wallet?* Jones thought. He was almost positive it was, but before he could be sure Old Chippy zipped up his leather jacket and started to laugh. I'm sorry about your pants, he said. But you gave me permission. I don't dispute that, said Jones, but I guess I didn't realize what I was getting into. Whoever does? said Old Chippy. Well, I suppose you're right about that, said Jones. But now that I let you do what you wanted, how about giving me a deal on some grass?

At Jones's question, Old Chippy backed away. He nodded to the leader, who then stepped forward. *Interesting how they delegate,* Jones thought. I should kick your ass for even proposing such a thing, said the leader. But it's nice out today and I spent last night banging out my old lady, so you've caught me in a good mood. I tell you what. Yes? said Jones. The leader pointed to Jones's wrist. I'll give you a 20 bag for your watch. *My watch?* Jones thought. His first impulse was to reject the idea. His watch had been a gift from his parents for completing college. It had an unusual green face and was powered kinetically by a small weight in the back. Jones had always treasured it. But there were his immediate needs to consider. Now that he was illiterate, it seemed unlikely that he would ever have a job again where a fancy watch like his would be useful.

OK, said Jones. You've got a deal. He took off his watch and tossed it to the leader. Then the leader pulled a plastic baggie out of his pocket and tossed it to Jones. He opened it and smelled the pot. Jones thought it smelled OK, but wasn't completely sure it was real so he turned back to the leader. Hey, said Jones, how do I know this is real? Would a man like me scam a man like you? said the leader. Well, said Jones, your colleague did just trick me into allowing him to cut apart my pants. His remark made the gang laugh, but Jones was determined to hold his ground. Usually I'd tell a pain in the ass like you to take a hike, said the leader, but considering our, well, extenuating circumstances, I guess I can make an exception just this one time. After all it is in every businessman's best interest to be just. The leader pulled out a small glass pipe from his jacket and turned to his gang. Boys, he said, keep a look out. At his words the gang scattered. He turned back to Jones. I tell you what, said the leader, I'll even pack it from my personal stash. Before Jones could protest and insist that he wanted to try the pot the punk had given him, the leader reached into his leather jacket and handed the packed pipe to Jones. He offered him a light. Jones put the pipe to his lips and inhaled. It tasted like pot but also somewhat strange. Instantly Jones felt high. What do you think? asked the leader. Jones noticed that the rest of the gang seemed to huddle around him. *Have they already returned from their lookout posts?* he wondered. And then he noticed that every man around him had a ridiculously big smile. Jones had to get out of there. He turned and faced the leader. It's good and strong, said Jones. He handed the pipe back to the punk. Excellent, said the leader. Hear that boys, another satisfied customer. Then all the punks started howling with a strange laughter that seemed to pulsate within Jones's head and extend outward into all the other amusement park sounds around him. *Suddenly*

I feel so strange, Jones thought. He didn't know what to do. Without another word, Jones turned away from the punks and resumed his journey to the beach.

CHAPTER 14: THE PSYCHIC

Jones ran as fast as he could through the amusement park, but with each step he took he grew more certain the leader of the punks had put something other than pot in his pipe. He couldn't put his finger on it exactly, but he felt a strange high coming on that he was unfamiliar with and suddenly everything around him started to change. Each person he passed seemed to give him dirty looks and Jones became more and more afraid. The cacophony of carousels and children's laughter appeared to be playing in sync with the beat of his heart, simultaneously pulling him closer to the beach and pushing him away. Bright lights swirled and blurred in the corner of his eyes. A little yellow. A flash of white. Clown faces and a little orange. A little red. A little blue. It was disorienting to be where he was so he just kept moving. The only thing for a man like him to do was move on.

Jones continued walking toward the beach with every ounce of strength he had and little by little he seemed to gain back more self-control. Gradually the lights and sounds bothered him less and eventually he spotted the boardwalk. It was only 100 yards away and just the sight of it elated him. He picked up his pace, but then out of nowhere he heard someone shout: Stop the illiterate!

Jones froze. Then he heard the same voice laugh. He spun around and spotted one of the punks leaning against a pole smoking a cigarette just 50 feet behind him, but the boy pretended not to see Jones. *That's strange,* Jones thought. He cut to his left. It wasn't the most direct route to the beach, but he couldn't take any chances. If he was being followed, his highest priority was evading the punks. But then he heard the voice again: Look at the cute little illiterate! Jones looked ahead and saw another punk. He was maybe 20 feet away and looked directly at Jones and smiled. *Just what are all these punks up to?* Jones wondered. He cut right down a makeshift back alleyway between the booths that housed the fortune-tellers and freak shows. But then he heard the voice, or rather voices this time: Hey, hey illiterate! It seemed to be coming from behind him and from somewhere up ahead. Silly illiterate, the voices continued. You'll never get away from us! Jones spun around. Behind him he saw three punks strolling toward him. He turned back around and started running forward, but then he stopped. Up ahead he saw three men. They were still far away, but one seemed to be wearing a cardigan sweater over a suit, one seemed to be wearing a smoking jacket over coveralls, and the last wore a tight black T-shirt and had a pair of dark glasses on that reflected the sun in the distance. Jones was paralyzed with fear. Instantly he thought: *The psychiatrist, the painter, and the bartender? Is it possible the conspirators have found me?* Jones spotted another alleyway on his left and sprinted down it. *If only there was a place to go,* Jones thought. *If only there was a place to hide.* Ahead of him he spotted a figure, a woman he thought, sticking her head out of the back of a booth. *Is she one of them?* he wondered. Jones didn't know if he should keep going or turn around.

But then she spoke. Hey, she said, you're in great danger. Jones skidded to a stop. And just how do you know that? he said. Because I'm a psychic, she said. A psychic? said Jones. Well really a psychic in training, said the woman. It's a long story, but please, come in here. Those punks are going to turn that corner any second and you don't need to be clairvoyant to know that young men running around these back alleys are never up to any good. Jones was impressed by her knowledge of the situation and followed her into the booth.

*

The psychic led Jones to a table adorned with tapestries that had a crystal ball in the middle. There were half a dozen chairs staggered around it. She offered one to Jones and took a seat across the table from him. I'm Sasha, she said, extending her hand. Nice to meet you, he said, I'm Jones. He shook her hand and looked into her eyes. *My, my, she's drop dead gorgeous,* Jones thought. Then he felt an erection coming on. So, said Jones, gesturing to the crystal ball on the table, is that what told you my life was in great danger? Not at all, said the psychic. I'm still in training so I don't know how to use this yet. Hmm, said Jones. I was out on the roof of my booth having a smoke. That's when I saw those punks messing with you. I watched them follow you after you walked away. Really? said Jones. *Then it actually happened and it wasn't just my imagination or the drugs after all,* he thought. Yeah, said the psychic. Maybe they thought the rips in your pants made you an easy target? I guess, said Jones, but I mean this is Coney Island. I'm sure there are vagrants walking around that would be easier to take down than me. But that's just the point, said the psychic. You're better-looking than most of the vagrants around here, so maybe the punks thought you might have some money? *Yes,* Jones thought, *I am better-looking than most of the vagrants around here.* He felt his confidence swell. He looked deeply into the psychic's eyes. I think the punks stole my wallet, he said. I think it was this fellow Old Chippy. But you don't know for sure? said the psychic. Well, it's a long story, said Jones, but the robbery occurred when I was asleep on the train. Ouch, said the psychic. Well maybe a reading would cheer you up? A reading? said Jones. Yeah, said the psychic, a reading. After all, I am trying to be a psychic. Oh, said Jones, you mean you want to tell my fortune? I'll save you the trouble. It turns out bad. So cynical, said the psychic. Clearly you've never dabbled with the occult before? I haven't, said Jones, but how can I be sure your reading will be accurate? I thought you said you were in training? Well everybody has to start somewhere, said the psychic. But how exactly does that work? asked Jones. How does what work? said the psychic. This whole training thing, said Jones. I mean you just said you don't know how to use a crystal ball, but you know how to give readings? Well, said the psychic, learning any trade takes time. How did you get into all this? said Jones. Because of my sister, said the psychic. This used to be her shop. Really? said Jones. Yeah, said the psychic. She used to be known as Madame Silvia. But she's not around any longer? asked Jones. Nope, said the psychic. Why not? asked Jones. It's sort of complicated, but basically one day she lost her ability to read minds. Instantly Jones was intrigued. What happened? he said. Well back in the day she was one of the biggest psychics in Coney Island. She was even voted the most insightful fortune-teller five years in a row. She gestured to some plaques hanging on the wall. I guess she was really good then? asked Jones. Allegedly, said the psychic. But then one day she wouldn't get out of bed. At first no one thought it was anything major. My parents just thought she was sick. But then that day in bed turned into a week in bed and then that week turned into a month. This was five years ago. I was 20 at the time and taking a few classes at a community college. I remember coming home one day and overhearing a conversation between my sister and her boyfriend. Our rooms shared a wall so I wasn't eavesdropping or anything. But I remember hearing my sister going on and on about how she couldn't do it anymore. Her boyfriend was this pushover who was always eager to help, so he kept insisting she tell him what was wrong. But my sister kept ignoring him, talking about one thing or the next, until finally she said she'd lost her psychic abilities. Really? said Jones. Yeah, said the psychic. Then my sister's boyfriend asked her what he could do for her, and she said he could get her as far away from Brooklyn as possible. The next morning she was gone. I haven't seen her since. What an incredible story, said Jones. I guess, said the psychic. What do you mean, you guess? asked Jones. Am I wrong to think that you're the one who now sounds cynical? Well the thing is, you sort of have to know my sister, said the psychic. I'm afraid I don't follow, said Jones. Well she was always really impulsive, said the psychic, and sort of a pathological liar. So I mean for all I know she could have just gotten bored with being a psychic and needed a change. Did you inherit her psychic abilities? asked Jones. I don't know, maybe, said the psychic. But this booth was already paid for, so I figured I should at least give it a shot. I can identify with your sister's situation, said Jones. Really? said the psychic. Yes, said Jones. A little over a week ago I woke up illiterate. And, you see, I'm a professional writer. Since discovering my condition my entire world has fallen to pieces and I've recently realized that nothing will ever be the same. Well that's not so bad, said the psychic, is it? What? said Jones. You don't think my illiteracy is bad? No, said the psychic. I don't mean to make light of your condition. I've never heard of anyone just waking up illiterate before. That must be horrible. It is, said Jones. I was talking about your realization, said the psychic. My realization? said Jones. Yeah, said the psychic. It's like that Sheryl Crow song. You know, that one "A Change Would Do You Good"? I suppose you're right, said Jones, but I don't know how I want to change. I don't know where I want my life to go. But you must, said the psychic. Jones noticed she was smiling at him and he got an idea. Why don't you tell me? he said. Me tell you? said the psychic. Yes, said Jones. How about that reading? OK, she said. Jones saw her blush and was thrilled she was responding to his advances. Stick out your hands, said the psychic. Stick out my hands? said Jones. Yeah, silly, said the psychic. Lay them across the table palm side up. Jones did as he was told. She reached across the table and placed her palms on top of his and Jones felt his erection grow. Now close your eyes and breathe deeply, said the psychic. Right now your body is releasing lots of conflicted energy. Internally it seems like you've been fighting yourself. *Well that's right on the money,* Jones thought. But in order to move forward you need to attain a sense of inner peace. You need to learn to listen to yourself and become the master of your emotions. You asked me to tell you where your life should go, but I can't tell you this. The only thing I can tell you is let your mind go and your body will follow. Now just breathe.

Jones continued to do as he was told. The breathing and the gentle sound of the psychic's voice relaxed him and sitting there with her he felt better than he had in days. He liked the advice she had given him. Let your mind go and your body will follow. He repeated this phrase over and over again. It was so true. It was so natural. It almost felt like something he had always known but had somehow forgotten. *Just think of all the grief I could have spared myself!* Jones thought. *Let your mind go and your body will follow. Such a well-written slogan.* He felt envious that he hadn't thought of it himself. He wondered how the psychic had thought of it. But then he stopped himself. In thinking such thoughts he was not letting his mind go, so instead Jones just concentrated on the words. He imagined them on a highway billboard. *Funny motivation for drivers,* he thought. Then he pictured them on a gigantic electronic sign and imagined some stranded motorist staring up at the flashing letters. He'd have to remember that scenario and maybe use it in one of his stories. Maybe he could even use the image as the basis for a novel. He wondered about the character of the stranded motorist. What kind of man would he be? The first person that came to mind was Steve Martin. *That's strange,* Jones thought. *Why am I thinking about Steve Martin at a time like this?* Then he grew enraged and opened his eyes.

That line, said Jones, it's plagiarized. You stole it from *L.A. Story.* What are you talking about? said the psychic. Let your mind go and your body will follow, said Jones. It's what the sign on the L.A. freeway tells Steve Martin in the movie. I don't know what you're talking about, said the psychic. Oh, come off it, said Jones. And frankly, the psychic continued, I find it insulting that you would accuse me of plagiarizing the advice I'm giving you during a psychic reading. But it's one of the most memorable lines in the entire movie, said Jones. I think Steve Martin's love interest says it too. What's her name? I think it might be Sara? It doesn't matter. She tells a story about some guy at a roller rink instructing her to skate that way. Let your mind go and your body will follow. That line sums up the entire existential point of the film!

The psychic was silent for a moment, so Jones stopped talking and studied her. She seemed to be retreating into herself and appeared to be on the verge of tears. She still looked stunning and he hadn't meant to hurt her feelings, but there were principles at stake. Fine, said the psychic. I'm sorry. You caught me. I did steal that line from *L.A. Story*. But why? asked Jones. Because it's one of my favorite movies, said the psychic. And it gives really good advice. That's true, said Jones. That film gives better advice than I could ever give, so I thought it would be OK to use it. Hearing that line just now did make me feel peaceful, said Jones. That was my only intention, said the psychic. I wasn't trying to deceive you. I understand, said Jones. For a moment he really wanted to. After accepting her apology Jones imagined himself standing up and embracing her. At his touch she would break down in tears. Then Jones would comfort her and make love to her on the very table that now stood between them. But then Jones realized that these thoughts were the same sorts of thoughts that had gotten him into so much trouble over the past few days. Had he not learned anything from chasing after Veronica? Then again, maybe the psychic was different? *She seems so kind,* Jones thought. He didn't know what he wanted to do, but Jones figured he could always come back and see the psychic later if he wanted to. Jones needed to sort out his own thoughts first. He stood up and decided to continue on to the beach.

I have to go, Jones said. But why? said the psychic. We've only just begun. Yes, I suppose we have, said Jones. But the thing is, I have a pressing engagement. An engagement? said the psychic. Yes, said Jones. Since I woke up I've been trying to go to the beach to sort out some things. Ever since you woke up? So by that you mean just now? said the psychic. You mean since you realized I'd plagiarized that line? No, said Jones. I meant it in a purely literal sense. Going to the beach to think was the first thought I entertained this morning when I woke up on the train. I'm so sorry for deceiving you, said the psychic. Then Jones heard her whimper and saw a tear roll down her face. *God, she really is lovely,* he thought. *Even when she's upset.* I didn't mean to hurt you, she continued. I didn't mean to cause you harm. I realize this, said Jones, and I really appreciate your trying to tell my fortune and everything, but I have some issues to resolve. You can't just leave, she said. You just can't! I'm afraid I can, said Jones. And I have to. But I sense such a strong connection between us! *So now her psychic powers suddenly seem to be working?* Jones thought. Listen, he said, let me go now, but maybe I'll come by later on and we can go get a cup of coffee or something. Really? said the psychic. You'll come back? It's possible, said Jones, and it's also possible I won't. Recently I've been in a lot of trouble. There's even a chance I may be wanted by the police. Oh no! said the psychic. The police? So in my absence you might want to reconsider this connection you feel between us, said Jones. You might not want to have anything to do with a man like me. So you really doubt my perception of us?

said the psychic. Do I doubt your perception? said Jones. Christ, just a few minutes ago you admitted to being a phony psychic!

Jones hadn't meant to say what he said. But he was frustrated and it just slipped out. His comments caused the psychic to start sobbing again and Jones decided that the best thing for him to do was leave. Well maybe I'll see you later, he said. The psychic just stared at him and didn't utter a single word. *God, she still looks so stunning,* Jones thought. Then he nodded to her and walked out the door.

CHAPTER 15: THE EX-DETECTIVE

As he walked away from the psychic's Jones felt more depressed than he had all day. He had felt affection for the psychic, but even she was an impostor. He was disappointed with himself and figured the best thing to do would be to continue on toward the beach and take his chances with the weed the punks had sold him. Up ahead he spotted a trash can, so he stopped and looked through its contents until he found a small aluminum can. *Perfect,* Jones thought. It wasn't crushed so he figured he could turn it into a pipe for his pot. He went through his jacket and found a lighter. Finally things seem to be looking up for him. But then out of nowhere a tennis ball hit him from behind. It smacked him in the middle of the back. Jones stopped and turned toward the direction he thought the ball must have come from. No one was there, so he figured it must just be kids horsing around and continued toward the beach. Then a second ball hit him. This one beaned him in his ear. The blow stung and Jones spun around in anger. Who's out there? he shouted. He still didn't see anyone behind him, so he continued walking. He tried to move faster and kept his head low. If he was correct, just up ahead he'd be able to turn out of the alley back into the amusement park and from there it was a straight shot to the boardwalk. But then Jones felt something hit him in the back again. *Was that a rock?* he wondered. Then something smashed into a signpost nearby and clanked to the ground. It was definitely a rock. Then a few more rocks and tennis balls flew toward him. In the distance somewhere he heard someone yell: Get the illiterate! And then: laughter, just horrible, hideous laughter. Jones spun around and took cover behind a trash can. Behind him he saw about half a dozen punks walking up the alley. *Should I run for it or try to hide and wait for them to pass?* he wondered. *But what if they see me?* In the alley he'd be done for, but back out in the amusement park he might have a chance.

Jones jumped up from behind the trash can and started running as fast he could down the alley toward the amusement park. Look at the illiterate go, said one punk. It's like he still thinks he has a chance. Then Jones heard more laughter and felt another rock hit him in the back. When he reached the end of the alley he turned into the amusement park. Jones looked back and saw that the punks were gaining on him. *Goddammit,* he thought. *All this just because I wanted to get high on the beach?*

Back in the amusement park Jones continued to run from the punks, but he had to be more careful now because the park was full of people. Jones tried to be cautious because he didn't want to seem suspicious and give anyone cause to stop him. He certainly didn't want to deal with the police. The only thing he wanted to do was to make it to the beach. *If the punks follow me there, so be it,* he thought. *Maybe I'll just have to take a swim?* Jones navigated his way through the crowds of people lined up in front of the games and the rides and the freak shows. Everyone there seemed to be in a daze. *It's like they're all on drugs,* Jones thought as he stepped around child after child. The punks were right behind him, though there seemed to be less of them now. Jones worried that they had spread out. But at least the crowds made them stop throwing rocks and tennis balls. The boardwalk was getting closer. Jones could see it up ahead and told himself to hang in there just a little longer.

Then out of nowhere someone threw a beer in his face. Jones was confused and stopped for a moment. He looked around him and saw that he was standing outside a concession stand, so he guessed maybe someone had just tripped and their beverage had accidentally hit him. But then Jones heard more laughter and recognized it. He looked up behind the bar. *Was that the bartender?* Jones thought. He wasn't sure. The man behind the bar at the concession stand didn't seem to recognize him. He didn't say anything to Jones. He just stood there, smiling. Then he laughed. Jones turned around and ran away from the concession stand. But then he realized that he was headed toward the punks. Chase him to the freak! they yelled. Jones skidded to a stop and took off toward the rides. It wasn't the most direct way to the boardwalk, but Jones had to get away from the bartender and the punks. But instead of diminishing, the bartender's laughter grew. *Maybe that's just the punks?* Jones hoped. Then he slipped on something and fell to the ground. As Jones stood up, he saw that he had slipped on motor oil. *Probably just from the rides,* Jones thought. He looked back to the punks. They were gaining on him again. He was standing near the Ferris wheel. He noticed that a man in coveralls working on the wheel was staring at him. *Had he thrown the oil?* Jones wondered. *But why?* Jones moved closer to the wheel and the man started to laugh. *But wait, could that be the mechanic?* he wondered. Jones turned back toward the boardwalk. He started sprinting. It was just a few feet away. He felt elated when he stepped onto the boards.

Jones's first instinct was to rush to the edge of the boardwalk and hop the railing down into the sand, but there was a punk waiting for him on the beach. *You've got to hand it to these punks for being so organized,* he thought. Jones started running west down the boardwalk, but the crowds made this difficult. The punks were still right behind him. *Don't any of these people find it a little bit unusual to see a grown man being chased by a gang of punks in broad daylight?* Jones thought. Then he heard another laugh. Jones turned around. At first nothing struck him out of the ordinary. But then he saw a face-painting stand set up on the boardwalk. He noticed that the face painter was staring at him, laughing. *Was that the painter?* Jones wondered. *Or maybe it was the capitalist in disguise?* Jones wasn't certain and continued to run, but it was only seconds before he slipped on something. He felt his legs go under him. Then Jones hit the boards hard with his hands.

The punks surrounded him. Jones looked up and recognized the leader. He saw Old Chippy too. He froze with fear. Old Chippy winked at him and flashed an X-Acto knife. *I guess this is just what it comes down to,* Jones thought. *Somehow my fate is to be killed by a bunch of punks outside an amusement park paces away from the beach?* He guessed he could try to fight them, but he was exhausted and didn't see the point.

Jones sat on the boards and stared up at them ready for the first blow. Then he heard someone shout: You punks! Get out of here! Leave that man alone! At first the punks laughed and flashed their blades at the man who had called them out, but the man didn't back down. He was large middle-aged fellow. His considerable paunch showed through a greasy wifebeater and he wore a porkpie hat. As he got closer Jones realized he was holding a gun. The punks started yelling, but the man came even closer. Get the hell away from my business! he shouted. Then Jones watched as he pointed the gun at the punks and smiled. The punks were smiling too. Something felt off to Jones. *It's almost as if my rescue has been staged,* he thought. But then the punks walked away. Jones didn't complain.

The man walked up to Jones and helped him to his feet. Are you all right? he said. Yeah, said Jones, just a little banged up, but nothing's broken. That's good, said the man. Thanks a million, said Jones. Think nothing of it, said the man. Well I appreciate it, said Jones, extending his hand. I'm Jones. Nice to meet you, said the man. I'm Mahoney. Thanks for defending me with your, uh, piece, said Jones. I hope you don't get in trouble for pulling it out here in public and all. Don't be silly, said the man. This is only a paintball gun. A paintball gun? said Jones. I thought it was real. Well even if it had been, there wouldn't be any trouble either, said the man. I know people. Really? said Jones. Yeah, said the man. I used to be a detective, but I don't do that anymore. I still have friends on the force, though, who understand a man's right to protect his place of business. Your business? said Jones. Yes, said the ex-detective. Perhaps you've heard of me? Then he gestured upward at a sign above a shooting range next to them. Jones looked up, but of course he couldn't read it. Surely you must have heard of the one and only *Shoot the Freak,* the ex-detective continued. For a mere three dollars any man, woman or child can shoot this here paintball gun at a live human target. No kidding, said Jones. Maybe this is just the place for me. Jones looked back at the ex-detective and saw that he seemed oddly pleased with what he had just said, so he shrugged his shoulders and both men shared an awkward laugh.

*

Jones thanked the ex-detective again for his help and started back toward the beach. It was only 20 feet away. But then he felt the man's hand on his shoulder. Jones's first instinct was to brush it away and keep on heading to the sand. But the ex-detective had shown him a good turn, so Jones figured he should see what he wanted. Yes? said Jones. What's the rush? said the ex-detective. Perhaps you'd care for a beer? A beer? said Jones. Beer was the last thing on his mind, but after running from the punks maybe it was the perfect thing. This one's on me, said the ex-detective. Then he opened a cooler under his cash register. He grabbed two tallboys and handed one to Jones. Thanks, he said. Please, think nothing of it, said the ex-detective. I want to make sure you're OK with what just occurred. What do you mean? asked Jones. As a local businessman, it reflects badly on all of us when something like that happens, said the ex-detective. I don't think you have any control over who those punks decide to chase, said Jones. Of course not, said the ex-detective, but it especially looks bad when their victim is someone not from around here. You can tell, huh? said Jones. Well, I really appreciate what you did. It looks even worse when the victim is a man like you, the ex-detective continued. A man like me? said Jones. Yes, said the ex-detective. There's nothing to be ashamed about being down on your luck. Oh, said Jones with a chuckle, you think I'm a vagrant because my pants are shredded and I probably smell like beer? Son, it's nothing to be ashamed of, said the ex-detective. I know I seem pretty flush now, but I battled homelessness myself for years. Sir, said Jones, let me explain. At one point things got so bad I was living under the boardwalk over in the Far Rockaways, the ex-detective continued. Really? said Jones. Yeah, said the ex-detective. It's no way for any man to live. Why is that? said Jones. Because living that way makes a man feel as if they're the last man on earth, said the ex-detective. In a way that sounds almost peaceful, said Jones. Well that was my initial intention. What was? asked Jones. Finding peace, said the ex-detective. That's why you became homeless? said Jones. The idea was to get rid of all my possessions and walk away from my life in order to make a fresh start, said the ex-detective. I see, said Jones. Just like people are always doing in the movies? Yeah, said the ex-detective, just like the movies. But why start over? said Jones. Did something happen? It's complicated, said the ex-detective. As I said, I used to be a detective. But one morning I woke up unable to do police work any longer. Really? said Jones. What exactly do you mean by that? What do I mean by what? said the ex-detective. I'm curious about how your inability developed, said Jones. You wouldn't describe what happened to you as a sort of illiteracy, would you? Not at all, said the ex-detective. I became a cop to save people, but after fifteen years on the force I realized that people don't want to be saved; they only want to shoot. I'm not sure I follow? said Jones. Well you should, said the ex-detective. It's not that complicated. It doesn't matter what you do. The violence never stops. Some people want to shoot themselves. Others shoot the people they hate or the people they love. Some even shoot people they don't know. Once I arrested one guy who shot some other guy because he thought shooting this other guy would make him famous. And everybody loves to shoot at the police and because of the police. Wait a minute, said Jones. People shoot because of the police? Yes, said the ex-detective. Because the police enforce the law and people resent having to abide by it. So you think having police actually contributes to crime and violence? said Jones. Yes, said the ex-detective. People either fear the police or hate the police. Just the sight of a man walking around with a gun, a badge, and the authority to arrest whomever he wants makes men do irrational things. I suppose that makes sense, said Jones. You know we come from animals? said the ex-detective. What? said Jones. Evolution, said the ex-detective, perhaps you've heard of it? Sure, said Jones. But maybe you don't know how it works? said the ex-detective. I understand how evolution works, said Jones. Oh, said the ex-detective, well even better. I believe that the entire idea of the police is flawed because it disrupts the higher order of things. But isn't that the point of it? said Jones. Isn't policing about protecting people from having to compete in the whole survival-of-the-fittest struggle? At its onset, yes, said the ex-detective, but in a modern-day context I think police make this struggle much worse. How? said Jones. Well for starters, internal corruption causes officers to take advantage of innocent people, which makes the support base for law enforcement diminish. Factor in the bureaucracy involved with actually getting anything done and the brazen ways professional criminals have come up with to get away with their crimes and you have the same society that pays taxes to support law enforcement simultaneously plagued by paranoia and distrust. Just try to think of even one acquaintance of yours who has never had a bad word to say about the police. I see your point, said Jones. Christ, even cops think badly of other cops. I can't even begin to describe what it's like working within those ranks other than to say that it's nothing short of being entirely surreal. Really? said Jones. Yeah, said the ex-detective. But I was young and naïve when I first took the job. Personally I'd always been a pacifist, so the idea was to extend my own beliefs into the community where I was assigned in the hope of making the city a better place for everyone. But that didn't work out? said Jones. Nothing ever does, said the ex-detective. As a rookie I was stationed in one of the worse precincts in the city. It was basically all housing projects and our main role was doing stop and frisks. I guess the idea was that maintaining a constant presence would discourage crime, but I noticed that on the days we patrolled the crime stats seemed to go up and on the days we didn't they were lower. Finally I started asking around and found out that there was this man Mr. Mackey who basically ran things in that neighborhood. The narcotics boys were sure he was a major drug lord, but no one could get close enough to him to know for sure. According to homicide, whenever anything went down people had to answer to him. So you see, even back then the absurdity of the police in an evolutionary context struck me. There I was working in a neighborhood where we were not needed. Our presence there upset the natural order of things. Clearly Mr. Mackey was the fittest among those people to lead. He climbed to the top of the evolutionary tower. But our being there confused people and caused them to act out and do rash things. I see, said Jones. Did you do anything about it? Did you try to make a change? Unfortunately I was reassigned before I had a chance to do much in that neighborhood, said the ex-detective. Oh, said Jones. After I left that assignment I talked to a bunch of veteran officers about my concerns and most just told me everything would work itself out eventually. But things got worse. By the time I made detective, I became indifferent to it all. Every day was the same and I barely paid attention to my work. It's a grueling experience, you know, to live your life knowing what you do doesn't matter. I agree, said Jones. It was only a matter of time before I had a nervous breakdown. What happened? said Jones. One day my partner and I drove up to the Bronx to investigate a homicide, but when we arrived at the crime scene I couldn't get out of the car. Wow, said Jones. I guess it all caught up to me that day, said the ex-detective. My body just couldn't take it any longer. I had to stop contributing to the cycle of endless violence. So what did you do? said Jones. Before I did anything the department sent me to see a shrink, said the ex-detective. I mean it's not every day that a decorated fifteen-year homicide detective won't get out of his car. That's true, said Jones. But you know how shrinks are, said the ex-detective. They don't really get it. I just had an awful experience with a psychiatrist myself, said Jones. Well mine wasn't necessarily awful, said the ex-detective. But he just didn't understand. Everything I'd done made perfect sense to me, but it didn't make sense to the shrink. After going to see him daily for six weeks the only useful thing the man ever said to me was that when a man thinks that his existence has become meaningless the time has come to change. So that's what I did. The next day I blew off my appointment with the shrink. I decided the best thing for me to do was to get off the grid for a little while, so I threw away all my possessions and stopped paying my rent. All it took was a few weeks before I was out on the streets. That seems a little drastic, said Jones. Not at all, said the ex-detective. Right away I realized that I needed to eliminate all traces of my former life in order to be able to resist the temptation to return to it. I needed to become anonymous. And in New York City what better way to do such a thing than by moving onto the streets? I guess you have a point, said Jones. So that's what I did, said the ex-detective. At first I stayed in Manhattan. I lived with other homeless people in the parks and survived by picking through the trash of fancy restaurants. But there were still so many people around, and after a while living this way felt oppressive too, so eventually I packed up my junk and moved out to Rockaway Beach. Really? said Jones. Yeah, said the ex-detective. I needed to go somewhere remote and peaceful where I'd be able to think about how my life had changed and figure out what I wanted to do next. So I went out there and lived on a deserted beach way out on the eastern end. For the first week I barely left my campsite. I just sat there on the sand, day and night, gazing at the sea. There I was, you know? I wanted to convince myself that my new reality was the only one that mattered. You see, I was afraid of accidentally speaking about my old life when I started meeting new people again. But you're speaking of it now? said Jones. Yes, said the ex-detective, but some things have changed. Now I'm more comfortable doing so. But back then I resolved to tell people only that I'd fallen on hard times because of the recession. I needed to eliminate all temptation to regress so I vowed never to speak of my career as a detective. Those were my rules and after a week of solitude I reentered the world. I took long walks from my camp down to the boardwalk to the west and then would loop back through the streets. I'd take this walk two or three times a day and sometimes I'd go fishing at the other end of the island. It was hard at first. What was? said Jones. Getting used to the reality that this was my life, said the ex-detective. But after I did, I treasured it. Gradually I befriended the locals and other beach walkers. Proprietors of restaurants offered me their leftovers and a few times I even sold the fresh fish I caught to those establishments. Around the Rockaways I became known as Captain Mahoney. Whenever anybody asked me where I was from I'd just point to the sea. Those were great times for me psychologically, but physically, I'm sure you can understand living without a home is hard. Of course, said Jones. After a while I started thinking about getting a job that would bring me in just enough to get a little place of my own out there. What kind of job? said Jones. Well it actually turned out to be the job I have now, said the ex-detective. Running *Shoot the Freak*? asked Jones. Well, more or less, said the ex-detective. One of the old-timers I fished with was this guy Doc and one day I was telling him how I was looking for work and he mentioned that he happened to own *Shoot the Freak* and could use a little help. Really? said Jones. Yeah, said the ex-detective. So the next day I went to work with him, but on our way here in the car I worried I'd made a mistake. I mean there I was on my way to work at a place that encouraged people to shoot at other human beings. I was concerned that just the act of shooting and spending my day watching people shoot would bring back all the memories I'd tried so hard to get rid of. But, a job is a job, right? Sure, said Jones. So I just tried to focus on how nice it would be to sleep inside again when it rained. When we got here I helped Doc open up and then he ran the register and I maintained the paintball guns. At least he didn't start you as the freak, said Jones. We had a local vagrant to do that, said the ex-detective. Really? said Jones. Did you shoot at him each morning to warm him up? Of course not, said the ex-detective. I can see you're a little critical of what we do here. I don't mean to give you a hard time or anything, said Jones, but I think shooting at a live human target encourages violence. I used to feel the same way, said the ex-detective. What made you change? asked Jones. Watching people shoot at the freak. Instead of finding anger or malice in their faces I saw relaxation and ease. Come on, said Jones. I find that a little hard to believe. I'm serious, said the ex-detective. There's something therapeutic about shooting a gun. Well I guess you have a point, said Jones. And when people walk away after they're finished shooting, said the ex-detective, their faces are always bursting with relief. You should give it a try. Take a few practice shots. I don't know, said Jones. I'm serious, said the ex-detective. Shooting the freak could change your life!

Before Jones had a chance to protest, the ex-detective turned toward the shooting range and pulled a lever that released a large bucket of water onto the middle of the shooting gallery. A man wearing a Halloween monster mask and a great deal of padding jumped up among the targets. Jones noticed he was soaking wet. Why'd you drench him like that? Jones asked. I needed to wake the freak up for your practice shots, said the ex-detective. But couldn't you have just called his name? said Jones. No, said the ex-detective. It's hard for him to hear with that mask on. Oh, said Jones. And besides, he knows he's not supposed to be sleeping on the job, said the ex-detective. Just think how it makes me look if someone comes here eager to shoot only to find the freak sleeping. The water keeps him on edge. Then the ex-detective handed Jones a paintball gun. Thanks, said Jones, but this really isn't necessary. Don't be silly, said the ex-detective. Well I guess a few shots would be OK, said Jones.

Jones took the gun from the ex-detective and walked up to the range. He aimed at the freak and pulled the trigger. He missed and saw the paintball he shot explode onto a trash can just to the freak's right. It's harder than it looks, said the ex-detective. Yeah, said Jones, I thought I aimed perfectly. Well we've messed with the sights on those guns a little, said the ex-detective. What? said Jones. You've rigged the guns? Not entirely, said the ex-detective. But they're off just a little bit. I'm sure you can understand. We do it for the freak. It's more humane that way. I see, said Jones. He took another shot and missed again, but this time he was close enough to make the freak jump out of his way. Just to show he was a good sport he took one final shot, but he failed to hit the freak this time as well. Jones felt an odd satisfaction shooting the gun. *Maybe there is some truth in what the ex-detective says?* Jones thought. Then he handed the gun back to the ex-detective.

You shouldn't feel bad about missing, said the ex-detective. The freak is nearly impossible to hit. Really? said Jones. Yeah, said the ex-detective. In a way knowing that made my initial experience working here with Doc easier. I see, said Jones. Does he still work here too? No, said the ex-detective. Unfortunately he passed away. I'm sorry to hear that, said Jones. It was tragic, said the ex-detective. But in a way Doc's death was the best thing that's ever happened to me. I thought you said he was your friend, said Jones. He was, said the ex-detective. I worked with him here for over two years. The man even let me sleep on his couch until I had enough money to get a place of my own. He taught me everything I know about the shooting boardwalk game business and was like a father to me. When he passed I was mortified. At first I didn't know how to go on. I just kept coming here each day and working as if Doc were still around, even though technically I guess I was working for free. I even started to pay the freak out of my own pocket. But then one day a lawyer showed up. A lawyer? said Jones. Yeah, said the ex-detective. Apparently Doc left a will. Really? said Jones. Yeah, said the ex-detective. The lawyer informed me that Doc had left me his business. And on that day my life changed. So you run everything now? said Jones. Yep, said the ex-detective. Well that's really some story, said Jones. Glad you think so, said the ex-detective. Now my own homelessness is a distant relic of my past, but I'll never forget my struggle. It sounds like you went through a lot, said Jones. I'm grateful to have lived through it all, said the ex-detective. I've always felt that experience keeps us grounded. That's true, said Jones. And I've always felt that it is important to honor my experience, said the ex-detective. Since I've taken over this here establishment, I only hire homeless vagrants to work as the freak. It's sort of my own little personal crusade. I'm sure they all appreciate the opportunity to work, said Jones. That's the idea, said the ex-detective. I want to give men down on their luck another chance to participate in the world again. Well that's nice of you, said Jones. In fact, we're looking for a few more freaks right now. If I think of anyone I'll send them your way, said Jones. But what about you? asked the ex-detective. Me? said Jones. Yeah, said the ex-detective. There's no shame in this work. Just look at yourself. You need to start somewhere. Sure, said Jones, but I think there's been a misunderstanding. Right now I'm not really looking for work. All day I've just been trying to go get high on the beach. Drugs are never the answer, said the ex-detective. I know, said Jones. But I'm not talking about doing drugs. I'm just talking about smoking a little pot and listening to the waves. Well I'm a little disappointed to hear that, said the ex-detective. You can't be serious? said Jones. Here I am going out of my way to help you, the ex-detective continued, only to hear you say thanks but no thanks and walk away? I appreciated your telling me your story, said Jones, but I never said I was available to work for you. And then there's the matter of that beer I gave you, said the ex-detective. You know they're not free? But you offered it to me, said Jones. And perhaps we should talk about those practice shots too, said the ex-detective. Paintballs don't grow on trees. What are you talking about? said Jones. Well if you don't want to accept my offer, please don't let me stop you from doing drugs on the beach, said the ex-detective. But I think we need to settle up your tab first. My tab? said Jones. Yeah, said the ex-detective. Just because I like you I'll let the beer slide, but by my count you took three shots, which at three dollars a pop means you owe me nine dollars. I thought they were free? said Jones. Free? said the ex-detective. Ha! What's free in this world? But you practically shoved the gun into my hands, said Jones. I only took them to be polite. Why you thought these things or took those shots is not my concern, said the ex-detective. As a businessman I'm only interested in the fact that you owe me nine dollars. The ex-detective pointed to a sign above the register. The price of each shot is clearly marked, he said. Can't you read? Then the ex-detective laughed. Jones wasn't sure what to do, but the more he thought about it, the less he felt any obligation to this man. Without another word he turned to walk away.

I wouldn't do that if I were you, said the ex-detective. Jones stopped and turned around to face him. And why not? he said. Why should I allow you to trick me into working for you as the freak? Hold on a minute, said the ex-detective. I haven't been trying to deceive you. I'm just an honest businessman asking for what I feel is rightfully mine. Honest? said Jones. I don't know about that. And now I'm giving you the opportunity to work off your debt. I'm not trying to trick you or threaten you. I haven't said that if you don't pay me I'll call up some of my old buddies from my detective days and have you arrested, though I could if I wanted. You'd have me arrested for just nine dollars? asked Jones. I haven't said that I'll flag down a cop right here on the boardwalk, the ex-detective continued, and say, I don't know, that you most likely have drugs in your pocket, have I? Wait a second, Jones started to say, but then he stopped. He was confused. How had he let this man put him in such a compromised position? Listen, said the ex-detective, it won't be so bad. You only owe me nine bucks, so I doubt it'll take you more than an hour or two of work. It's not our busiest time of year, but I'll pay you five cents every time someone shoots at you, so after 180 shots you're free to go. And who knows, maybe you'll even enjoy it; many do. Some even rave that being the freak is the ultimate form of exercise. Then the ex-detective went on, but Jones stopped listening.

He gazed out at the ocean. *If only, if only, if only*, Jones thought. *If only I wasn't here. It's as if the whole city has conspired against me.* Then Jones started thinking about his illiteracy. He wished it had never happened, but then he stopped himself. Jones realized his old life didn't matter anymore. Neither did his current life. Nothing did. Even still, he wished he hadn't tried to score pot and had just walked to the beach. *But maybe something else would have happened?* After all, he didn't seem to be having the best of luck these days. *If only I hadn't talked to the punks*, Jones thought. Then he saw them again.

Jones began to tremble as he watched the punks walk toward him from the beach onto the boardwalk. They stopped at the entryway, as if they were guarding a post. *Something about this isn't right*, Jones thought. It seemed like they were laughing. He heard the ex-detective laugh too and turned to him. You set me up, you son of a bitch, said Jones. And so what if I did? asked the ex-detective. Well did you or didn't you? said Jones. Does it really matter? said the ex-detective. I guess not, said Jones. He wanted to figure out a way to escape away from the boardwalk and maybe even the city, but since the punks had returned he reasoned that there was no point in running. It seemed like he'd have to run the gauntlet before he could be free.

Jones walked over to the mini refrigerator below the register and grabbed himself another beer. Hey, said the ex-detective, what do you think you're doing? Add it to my tab, said Jones. The ex-detective smiled. Of course, he said. Well, let's get on with it then, said Jones. I'm ready to be the freak. Then the ex-detective nodded and gestured for Jones to follow him down into the shooting gallery.

CHAPTER 16: RUNNING THE GAUNTLET

At first there was nothing, just a strange sense of awareness. But then Jones heard a creak overhead. And then: a gush of cold. Jones was suddenly awake. *Was it possible?* he thought. *Did I actually fall asleep?* When he'd entered the shooting gallery the ex-detective had told him to make himself comfortable until they got their first customer, so he sprawled out on top of a bench. *But sleep? Unbelievable,* Jones thought. *Who could sleep in a situation like this? Apparently I can.*

Jones tried to look at his watch but then he remembered that he had traded it to the punks for drugs. Outside it seemed that night had fallen. *Have I really spent my entire day in Coney Island?* he wondered. *Who would have thought?* Suddenly Jones heard a popping sound and then another bucket of water fell on him. Goddammit! he yelled. He shivered with cold. Then he heard: Ladies and gentleman, that should drive the freak out of his hole, especially on a chilly night like this. And then all he heard was laughter. *Well I guess the time has come to run the gauntlet and work off my debts,* Jones thought. Then he put on the mask the ex-detective had given him and walked around the back partition into the shooting gallery.

There he is, ladies and gentlemen, Jones heard the ex-detective say over the loud speaker. Go ahead and take a shot, he continued. That's right, unleash your fury on the freak! And with those words Jones heard the pop of the paintball guns. At first he wasn't sure what to do, so he looked up at the shooters. He figured it would be a slow night, but the range was full and all ten shooting spots were occupied. *Well at least I'll pay off my debts faster this way,* Jones thought. The paintballs rained down on him and Jones started trying to dodge them. He hopped to the right and then to the left and then dove behind a barrier before jumping out again. Moments later the first one caught him in the left ear with so much force that it made him spin around. Jones dove to the ground for a moment to collect himself. Up above he heard the shooters laugh. And then he heard the ex-detective say: Come on, freak! Face your conspirators! The time has come for you to be a man! *Did he just say conspirators?* Jones wondered. *No, it's not possible.* He looked up at the range to try to see the people who were shooting at him, but the spotlights shining on him from above made it impossible to see any of their faces. I'm not paying you to sit around! yelled the ex-detective over the loudspeaker. *Well, I guess he's right,* Jones thought. *I guess I need to suck it up and get this over with.*

Jones stood up and started running patterns back and forth through the gauntlet from barrier to barrier. He was quick, but with each pass he received at least one or two body shots. Every time he was hit he heard more people laugh. It sounded as if the shooters were all drunk. *They probably are,* Jones guessed. *After all you'd have to be wasted to enjoy a thing like this.* But then Jones remembered that not long ago he had enjoyed shooting the gun too. He felt ashamed.

Then the shooters started shouting at him. Jones heard: I just hit the freak. And then: Get that motherfucker! And then: He's so slow. Think he's really just some bum? And then: Jesus, I can't miss him. He keeps running right into my shots. And then: I know. Maybe he's just stupid? And then: Like a retarded illiterate. Jones tried to look toward the shooter who mentioned his condition, but then another paintball crashed into him, so he just kept running the gauntlet. He felt saddened by everything that was happening. *It's like I'm nothing,* Jones thought. *It's as if I were just a piece of trash. And why have I been made to feel this way? Just because I woke up one day unable to read? Just because I stumbled into something that challenges the understanding of others? Well maybe that's their fault and not mine. Maybe it's the fault of this entire goddamn city for being more concerned with sustaining itself than with being able to understand. After all, they're just like me!*

Jones jumped on top of one of the barriers in the shooting gallery. He raised his arms up in the air and shouted: Fuck you! He pointed at the shooters and swung his arm from man to man. Fuck you and you and you! You hear that? said one shooter. Did the freak just tell us to go fuck ourselves? said another. What's the big idea? said another. I'm sorry, folks, said the ex-detective. He's not supposed to talk. Well that's messed up, said another shooter. There're kids around. How about five free shots each? said the ex-detective. Jones couldn't help himself anymore and started to laugh. *They're all just like me,* he thought. *An entire city of freaks either shooting or getting shot at.* Then a paintball hit Jones in the shoulder. He continued to laugh. Jones stayed on top of the barrier and stared straight into the blinding light up above. He thought of his conspirators and wondered what they would pretend to be shooting at and imagined them all before him again, standing shoulder to shoulder along the shooting range with their weapons raised and pointed at him. *I wonder who the psychiatrist would shoot?* Jones thought. *Maybe his wife? Or possibly the patient who stole her from him, the one who couldn't stop jerking off? Then again maybe the psychiatrist would shoot the President for causing the recession that forced him to move upstairs? Then Jones let out a long laugh. And what about the painter? Well that's an easy one. The painter would shoot the dealer who convinced him to take his work seriously and subsequently caused him to fail.* Jones felt a paintball hit him in the head, but he barely flinched. Nice shot, painter! yelled Jones back to the shooter. You can do better than that! More hatred! More power! Feel how inadequate you are! *And what about the capitalist?* Jones thought. *Maybe he'd go after charities? Or maybe he'd shoot the bankers who had more talent than him? Maybe he'd never lost his ability to make money at all, but his time had just passed? And the mechanic? Maybe he'd never been any good?* Jones thought. *Maybe he'd pretend to be shooting his useless hands? And what about that cranky ophthalmologist?* Jones thought. *Well maybe he'd shoot the publishers who had rejected his work and prevented him from being a writer. That's who his agent would probably shoot,* Jones thought. *And writers like me whose work she poured her energy into at the expense of her own.* Then he thought of his girlfriend. *And Caroline?* he wondered. *She'd shoot all the directors who never cast her and forced her to start writing. Because I'm sure she was sincere when she told me writing was really the only thing she's ever aspired to do,* Jones thought laughing even more. *And speaking of aspirations, what about my assistant? She'd probably shoot at me for standing in her way. And my editor? He'd probably shoot at me too because he envies my talent and success. Ah youth,* Jones thought. And then he pictured Veronica. Though he barely knew her, she'd seemed so angry. *Maybe she'd pretend to be shooting at everything. So would the bartender. And so would the punks.* A paintball hit Jones in the head again, but he held his ground. *And what about the neurologist?* Jones wondered. *Maybe the folks that caused his numerous nervous breakdowns? But in a way he seemed proud of them. So maybe he'd shoot whoever convinced him to modernize his office in such a ridiculous way?* Jones thought, amused by his memories of that place. *And what about the psychic who plagiarized his fortune?* He wasn't sure about her. Their meeting was brief and for the most part she seemed kind. *But then there was the fat blind woman at the bar?* Jones remembered. A paintball hit him square in the forehead. *Well she wouldn't shoot at anything, at least not intentionally, because after all she can't see.* He felt another paintball hit him in the head. It seemed to take something out of him. *And what about the little boy who burned his eyes out by staring into the sun? He'd probably shoot at everything intentionally. Such an angry young man,* Jones thought. A few more paintballs hit him in the head and Jones noticed he was starting to feel dizzy. *And what about New York City?* Jones thought, only half-lucidly. *What would good old Lady Liberty shoot at if she walked down from her high pedestal into this lowly shooting gallery?* Jones wondered. It occurred to him that in a way she was like the boy. *She'd shoot at everything intentionally,* Jones thought. *Because she's always been such an angry old city. Because at heart, she's just a miserable nihilist like everyone else.* Another paintball hit him in the head. Then he felt another hit his jaw. And then another. And another. He tried to keep laughing through it all but after a while he stopped and just tried to keep standing. It was only a matter of time before a final blow knocked Jones off the barrier back behind it and onto the ground.

Jones felt weak, but he was eager for his experience in the gauntlet to continue. *What more can they throw at me?* he wondered. *Surely my debt must be almost paid off by now?* He tried to stand back up, but then he sank back down to the dirt. *So dizzy,* he thought. Then he heard something and felt hands lifting him up under his armpits. He couldn't see who it was. He wanted to ask where they were taking him. But then: nothing. All around Jones everything faded to black.

CHAPTER 17: ESCAPE FROM NEW YORK

Jones came to a few hours later. He felt something cool on his right cheek and heard vibrations somewhere below. He opened his eyes and saw that he was in a car sitting next to the psychic. She was driving and Jones was in the passenger seat slouched against the window. He was relieved but at the same time afraid.

Finally he wakes up, said the psychic. Wait a minute, said Jones, but you're the psychic? Can you please call me Sasha? she said. Sorry, said Jones, but I don't understand what's happening. Whoever does? said the psychic. But I mean in a literal sense, said Jones. Just moments ago I was running the gauntlet as the freak and now I'm here with you in your car? Well you have been out for a little while now, said the psychic. I have? said Jones. Yes, said the psychic, for at least an hour I'd say. I think you took quite a few shots to the head and eventually passed out. I vaguely remember, said Jones. But how did you get me away from the ex-detective? The ex-detective? said the psychic. Yes, said Jones. He's the man who runs *Shoot the Freak*. Oh, said the psychic. After you went down, he started trying to convince the shooters to stay and shoot some more. I'd been watching you since you left my booth, so when I saw the moment was right I snuck you out the side door into my car. Did anyone see you? said Jones. I don't think so, said the psychic. But are you absolutely sure? said Jones. Of course not, said the psychic. But I don't think anyone has been following us. Jones shook with fear. Christ you're paranoid, said the psychic. I have my reasons, said Jones. We all do, said the psychic. But wait a second, said Jones. I don't understand any of this. So you've said, said the psychic. Why did you rescue me? said Jones. Because I felt bad about deceiving you earlier, said the psychic. Where are you taking me? asked Jones. Wherever you want to go, said the psychic, but I was sort of thinking about leaving this city for good. Leaving New York? said Jones. I thought you were trying to get your psychic business off the ground? I was, said the psychic, but I wasn't really ever any good at it. Just look at our session. That's true, said Jones. And besides, the psychic continued, I've always found it difficult to think about the future at the expense of the present. I can understand that, said Jones. And well, facts are facts, said the psychic. Right now I'm not happy doing what I'm doing and you needed to get away from those shooters and the punks, so I figured the best thing for us to do would be to leave. But we barely know each other, said Jones. It doesn't bother me if it doesn't bother you, said the psychic. Well I guess it doesn't, said Jones, but where will we go? I'm not sure, said the psychic. Do you have any ideas? Well, said Jones, the only thing I've wanted to do all day is to go get high on the beach. So why don't we go to one then? said the psychic. But we're at the beach right now, said Jones. We could go to another one? said the psychic. But where? said Jones. I don't know, said the psychic. How about Los Angeles? I hear Venice is beautiful this time of year. You want to drive all the way to L.A.? said Jones. Why not? said the psychic. Since I plagiarized that line from *L.A. Story* earlier, I can't seem to get California out of my head. Let your mind go and your body will follow? said Jones. It might be nice, said the psychic. Sure, but people don't just do things like that because they might be nice, Jones started to say, but then he stopped himself. Suddenly he felt taken by the idea. OK, said Jones. I'm game. Great, said the psychic. It's late so I'm not sure how far we'll get tonight but could you look at my map and tell me what you think? The psychic passed him the folded map and Jones froze.

Didn't I tell her about my illiteracy? Jones wondered. *Maybe I didn't mention it earlier? Maybe what I'm about to do is a horrible idea?* He thought of his old life. He thought of his girlfriend and his job and all the years he'd spent trying to make a name for himself in New York. He couldn't just abandon it all, could he? But the timing of this escape was certainly impeccable. And then there was the fact that he liked the psychic. Maybe he wasn't really happy doing what he was doing. He couldn't go on trying to figure out his illiteracy forever. Maybe he'd never really been happy living the way he had lived before waking up illiterate?

A million thoughts filtered in and out Jones's mind as he sat there holding the map. *It all has to stop,* he resolved. *There has to be an end to all this indecision.* He needed to stop thinking in fragments and start entertaining concrete thoughts again. He had to try to read the map because only through reading it would he be able to find a way out of this strange city, and maybe that's what he had been looking for all along. *A way out?* Jones thought. *Yes.* He turned on the interior light of the car and opened the map. He located Coney Island by the shape of the peninsula and tried to figure out where they were. And then: He was shocked. The street names appeared clear to him. It took Jones a minute or two to understand what was happening. Once again he was able to read.

Oh, said the psychic, I forgot about your condition. Sorry. We can pull over and I'll look at it myself. No need, said Jones. Do you know the best way then? asked the psychic. No, said Jones. But I don't seem to be illiterate any longer. What? said the psychic. It's true, said Jones. Then he read a few street names off the map. This is so strange. I don't understand why this is happening now. Well sometimes our bodies try to tell us things, said the psychic. Maybe you just figured out something important? It's possible, said Jones. My doctors always said that bit about our bodies trying to tell us things. But that was when I was illiterate. Well, said the psychic, what's different now?

But the truth was Jones didn't really know. There were physical changes like the awful state of his clothing and his exhaustion from running the gauntlet, but nothing overall that he could pinpoint. He was tempted to reconsider everything about his condition, but at the same time he didn't want to because he was more interested in where he was going than where he had been. Jones looked back to the psychic and held his finger to his lips. Then he looked back down at the map. After studying it for a few minutes he told her the route she should take and then he began thinking about towns where they could stop and rest once they made it past the city limits and eventually entered into Pennsylvania.

As they drove up the ramp onto the Verrazano Bridge Jones looked out the window behind him back at the city and watched it fade into the distance. Along the horizon the eastern sky was pink, and looming just above the Brooklyn skyline Jones spotted the sun. *So beautiful,* he thought as he turned back around to face the road. But then he stopped himself. He had to take one last look. Jones turned around and gazed at the sun. He realized it was rising.

ACKNOWLEDGEMENTS

A big thanks to Chris Lavergne, Mink Choi, and Mark Kupasrimonkol at Thought Catalog. Without you this book would not have been possible.

Thanks to Laura Carney, copy editor extraordinaire.

Thanks to all the people who published and programmed me: Steven Seighman and Shya Scanlon at *Monkeybicycle;* Mauro Carichni at *SPACEY;* Todd Zuniga at *Literary Death Match;* Jim Ruland at *Vermin on the Mount;* Susan Kirschbaum at *Lit Society No. 8;* Marco Rafala and Lee Goldberg at *Guerilla Lit;* Alison Weaver and Elsa Bermudez at *H.O.W. Journal.*

Thanks to my early readers, friends, and family who helped me along the way and the artists who have inspired me: Jason Napoli Brooks, Scott Geiger, Ryan Penny, TJ Noble, Marie and J Wall, Ben Bailey, Steve Froehlich, Claudia Payne, Scott Wilson, Dave Epstein, my sisters Emily, Stephanie, Erin, and Megan, Greg Bocquet, Jen Woodruff, Brad Crowley, Aaron Smith, Matt Stewart, Andrew Welder, Jeff Covey, Jay Kokernak, Josh Kahan, Dave Stoller, Gary Ford, Elizabeth Castoria, Yew Leong Lee, Andy Bodor and Cake Shop, Chaim Soutine, William

Faulkner, Bob Dylan, Roberto Bolaño, Franz Kafka, Fyodor Dostoevsky, Phillip K. Dick, Albert Camus, Crimpshrine, the Grateful Dead, Dinosaur Jr., Neil Young, Led Zeppelin, Cymande, and anyone who has ever come out to or read at The Enclave.

Thanks to Elizabeth Wurtzel for your edits and for being the most amazing wife ever.

And thanks to my parents Sarah and Jim, and to 104 Crimson Place; there will always be a part of this book in Pennsylvania.

ABOUT THE AUTHOR

Photograph by Ryan Penny

Jim Freed is the author of the novels *The Illiterate* and *The Unfulfilled*. His writing has appeared in the *New York Times, Monkeybicycle, H.O.W. Journal, SPACEY, Stereogum,* on *NPR (Neighborhood Public Radio)* in conjunction with the 2008 Whitney Biennial, and elsewhere. He lives in New York City where he curates The Enclave Reading Series. For more info go to: www.james-freed.com.